BALEFIRE

BOOK ONE
A CHALICE OF WIND

CATE TIERNAN

razOr
bill

Balefire 1: A Chalice of Wind

RAZORBILL

Published by the Penguin Group
Penguin Young Readers Group
345 Hudson Street, New York, New York 10014, U.S.A.
Penguin Group (USA) Inc., 375 Hudson Street, New York, New York 10014, U.S.A.
Penguin Group (Canada), 90 Eglinton Avenue, Suite 700, Toronto,
Ontario, Canada M4P 2Y3 (a division of Pearson Penguin Canada Inc.)
Penguin Books Ltd, 80 Strand, London WC2R 0RL, England
Penguin Ireland, 25 St Stephen's Green, Dublin 2, Ireland
(a division of Penguin Books Ltd)
Penguin Group (Australia), 250 Camberwell Road, Camberwell,
Victoria 3124, Australia (a division of Pearson Australia Group Pty Ltd)
Penguin Books India Pvt Ltd, 11 Community Centre, Panchsheel Park,
New Delhi - 110 017, India
Penguin Group (NZ), Cnr Airborne and Rosedale Roads, Albany,
Auckland 1310, New Zealand (a division of Pearson New Zealand Ltd)
Penguin Books (South Africa) (Pty) Ltd, 24 Sturdee Avenue,
Rosebank, Johannesburg 2196, South Africa

Penguin Books Ltd, Registered Offices: 80 Strand, London WC2R 0RL, England

10 9 8 7 6 5 4 3 2 1

Interior design by Christopher Grassi

Library of Congress Cataloging-in-Publication Data

Tiernan, Cate.
    A chalice of wind / Cate Tiernan.
        p. cm. — (Balefire ; 1)
    Summary: Separated since birth, seventeen-year-old twins Thais and
 Clio unexpectedly meet in New Orleans where they seem to be pursued
 by a coven of witches who want to harness the twins' magickal powers
 for its own ends.
    ISBN 1-59514-045-X
    [1. Witchcraft—Fiction. 2. Twins—Fiction. 3. Sisters—Fiction.
4. Immortality—Fiction. 5. New Orleans (La.)—Fiction.]
I. Title. II. Series.
PZ7.T437Cd 2005
[Fic]—dc22

                                                        2005008145

Printed in the United States of America

A shocking discovery . . .

Slowly I turned, finally face-to-face with the mysterious—

Me.

I blinked, and for one second I almost put up a hand to see if someone had slipped a mirror in front of me. My eyes widened, and identical green eyes widened simultaneously. My mouth opened a tiny bit, and a mouth shaped like mine but with slightly darker lip gloss also opened. I stepped back automatically and quickly scanned this other me, this Clio.

Our hair was different—hers was longer, I guessed, since it was in a messy knot on the back of her head. Mine was feathered in layers above my shoulders. She was wearing a white tank top and pink-and-red surfer shorts that laced up the front. She had a silver belly ring. We had the same long legs, the same arms. She had a slightly darker tan. We were the same height and looked like we were the same weight, or almost. And here was the really, really unbelievable part:

We had the exact same strawberry birthmark, shaped like a crushed flower. Only hers was on her left cheekbone, and mine was on the right. We were *identical*, two copies of the same person, peeled apart at some point to make mirror images of each other.

Even though my brain was screaming in confusion, one coherent thought surfaced: there was only one possible explanation.

Clio was my twin sister.

To Barry Varela, King of the Back Story and Plotman Extraordinaire. Thanks for everything.

Prologue

When the shades were down, you had to open the train compartment door to see who was inside. The last four minutes had taught us this as my friends Alison and Lynne and I raced through the train cars, looking for our trip supervisor.

"Not this one!" Alison said, checking out one compartment.

"Do you think it was something she ate?" Alison asked. "I mean, poor Anne. Yuck."

We were only on day three of our junior-year trip to Europe—having done Belgium in a whirlwind, we were speeding through Germany and would end up in France in another four days. But if Anne was really sick, she would be flown home. Maybe it was just something she ate. Our supervisor, Ms. Polems, could decide.

"Thais, get that one!" Lynne called, pointing as she looked through a compartment window.

I cupped my hands around my eyes like a scuba mask and pressed them against the glass. Just as quickly I pulled away as four junior-class pinhead jocks started catcalling and whistling.

"Oh, I'm so sure," I muttered in revulsion.

"Oops! *Entschuld—entschuh—*" Alison began in another doorway.

"*Entschuldigung!*" Lynne sang, pulling Alison back into the corridor.

I grinned at them. Despite Anne being sick, so far we were having a blast on this trip.

I seized the handle of the next compartment and yanked. Four tourists were inside—no Ms. Polems. "Oh, sorry," I said, pulling back. Two of the men stared at me, and I groaned inwardly. I'd already dealt with some over-friendly natives, and I didn't need more now.

"Clio?" one of the men said in a smooth, educated voice.

Yeah, right. Nice try. "Nope, sorry," I said briskly, and slid the door shut. "Not here," I told Alison.

Three doors up ahead, Lynne swung out into the corridor. "Found her!" she called, and I relaxed against the swaying train window, miles of stunning mountainy German landscape flashing by. Ms. Polems and Lynne hurried by me, and I slowly followed them, hoping Pats and Jess had tried to clean up our compartment a little.

Jules gazed silently at the compartment door that had just clicked loudly into place. That face . . .

He turned and looked at his companion, a friend he had known for more years than he cared to count. Daedalus looked as shocked as Jules felt.

"Surely that was Clio," Daedalus said, speaking softly so their seatmates wouldn't hear. He ran an elegant, long-fingered hand through hair graying at the temples, though still thick despite his age. "Wasn't Clio her name? Or was it . . . Clémence?"

"Clémence was the mother," Jules murmured. "The one who died. When was the last time you saw the child?"

Daedalus held his chin, thinking. Both men looked up as a small knot of students, led by an official-looking older woman, bobbed down the rocking corridor. He saw her again—that face—and then she was gone. "Maybe four years ago?" he guessed. "She was thirteen, and Petra was initiating her. I saw her only from a distance."

"But of course, they're unmistakable, that line," Jules said in an undertone. "They always have been."

"Yes." Daedalus frowned: confronted with an impossibility, his brain spun with thoughts. "She had to be the child, yet she wasn't," he said at last. "She really wasn't—there was nothing about her—"

"Nothing in her eyes," Jules broke in, agreeing.

"Unmistakably the child, yet not the child." Daedalus cataloged facts on his fingers. "Clearly not an older child, nor a younger."

"No," Jules said grimly.

The conclusion occurred to them at the same instant. Daedalus's mouth actually dropped open, and Jules put his hand over his heart. "Oh my God," he whispered. "Twins. Two of them! *Two!*"

He hadn't see Daedalus smile like that in . . . he didn't know how long.

3

This was so effing *frustrating*.

If I clenched my jaws any tighter, my face would snap.

My grandmother sat across from me, serenity emanating from her like perfume, a scent she dabbed behind her ears in the morning that carried her smoothly through her day.

Well, I had *forgotten* to dab on my freaking *serenity* this morning, and now I was holding this piece of copper in my left fist, my fingernails making angry half-moons in my palm. Another minute of this and I would throw the copper across the room, sweep the candle over with my hand, and just *go*.

But I wanted this so bad.

So bad I could taste it. And now, looking into my grandmother's eyes, calm and blue over the candle's flame, I felt like she was reading every thought that flitted through my brain. And that she was amused.

I closed my eyes and took a deep breath, all the way down to my belly ring. Then I released it slowly, willing it to take tension, doubt, ignorance, impatience with it.

Cuivre, orientez ma force. Copper, direct my power, I thought. Actually, not even thought—lighter than that.

Expressing the idea so lightly that it wasn't even a thought or words. Just pure feeling, as slight as a ribbon of smoke, weaving into the power of *Bonne Magie*.

Montrez-moi, I breathed. Show me.

You have to walk before you can run. You have to crawl before you can walk.

Montrez-moi.

Quartz crystals and rough chunks of emerald surrounded me and my grandmother in twelve points. A white candle burned on the ground between us. My butt had gone numb, like, yesterday. Breathe.

Montrez-moi.

It wasn't working, it wasn't working, *je n'ai pas de la force, rien du tout*. I opened my eyes, ready to scream.

And saw a huge cypress tree before me.

No grandmother. An enormous cypress tree almost blocked out the sky, the heavy gray clouds. I looked down: I still held the copper, hot now from my hand. I was in woods somewhere—I didn't recognize where. *Une cyprière*. A woodsy swamp—cypress knees pushing up through still, brown-green water. But I was standing on land, something solid, moss-covered.

The clouds grew darker, roiling with an internal storm. Leaves whipped past me, landed on the water, brushed my face. I heard thunder, a deep rumbling that fluttered in my chest and filled my ears. Fat raindrops spattered the ground, ran down my cheeks like tears. Then an enormous *crack!* shook me where I stood, and a simultaneous stroke of lightning blinded me. Almost

5

instantly, I heard a shuddering, splintering sound, like a wooden boat grinding against rocks. I blinked, trying to look through brilliant red-and-orange afterimages in my eyes. Right in front of me, the huge cypress tree was split in two, its halves bending precariously outward, already cracking, pulled down by their weight.

At the base, between two thick roots that were slowly being tugged from the earth, I saw a sudden upsurging of—what? I squinted. Was it water? Oil? It was dark like oil, thick—but the next lightning flash revealed the opaque dark red of blood. The rivulet of blood also split into two and ran across the ground, seeping slowly into the sodden moss, the red startling against the greenish gray. I looked down and saw the blood swelling, running faster, gushing heavily from between the tree roots. My feet! My feet were being splashed with blood, my shins flecked with it. I lost it then, covered my mouth and screamed into my tight palm, trying to move but finding myself more firmly rooted than the tree itself—

"Clio! Clio!"

A cool hand took my chin in a no-nonsense grip. I blinked rapidly, trying to clear rain out of my eyes. My grandmother was holding my chin in one hand and had her other under my elbow.

"Stand up, child," Nan instructed calmly. The candle between us had been knocked over, its wax running on the wooden floor. My knees felt wobbly and I was gulping air, looking around wildly, orienting myself.

"Nan," I gasped, swallowing air like a fish. "Nan, oh, *déesse*, that sucked."

"Tell me what you saw," she said, leading me out of the workroom and into our somewhat shabby kitchen.

I didn't want to talk about it, as if the words would recall the vision, putting me back into it. "I saw a tree," I said reluctantly. "A cypress. I was in a swamp kind of place. There was a storm, and then—the tree got hit by lightning. It got split in two. And then—blood gushed out of its roots."

"Blood?" Her gaze was sharp.

I nodded, feeling shivery and kind of sick. "Blood, a river of blood. And it split in two and started running over my feet, and then I yelled. Yuck." I trembled and couldn't help looking at my bare feet. Not bloody. Tan feet, purple-painted toenails. Fine.

"A tree split by lightning," my grandmother mused, pouring hot water into a pot. The steamy, wet smell of herbs filled the room, and my shivering eased. "A river of blood from its roots. And the river split in two."

"Yeah," I said, holding my mug in my cold hands, inhaling the steam. "That pretty much sums it up. Man." I shook my head and sipped. "What?" I said, noticing that my grandmother was watching me.

"It's interesting," she said in that way that meant there were a thousand other words inside her that weren't coming out. "Interesting vision. Looks like copper's good for you. We'll work on it again tomorrow."

"Not if I see you first," I muttered into my mug.

7

This isn't happening.

I could tell myself that a thousand times, and a thousand times the cold reality of my life would ruthlessly sink in again.

Next to me, Mrs. Thompkins gave my hand a pat. We were sitting side by side in the Third District Civil Court of Welsford, Connecticut. Two weeks ago, I had been happily scarfing down a *pâtisserie Anglaise* in a little bakery in Tours. Today I was waiting to hear a judge discuss the terms of my father's will.

Because my father was dead.

Two weeks ago, I'd had a dad, a home, a life. Then someone had had a stroke behind the wheel, and the out-of-control car had jumped a curb on Main Street and killed my dad. Things like that don't happen to people, not really. They happen in movies, sometimes books. Not to real people, not to real dads. Not to me.

Yet here I was, listening to a judge read a will I'd never even known existed. Mrs. Thompkins, who'd been our neighbor my whole life, dabbed at my cheeks with a lavender-scented hankie, and I realized I'd been crying.

"The minor child, Thais Allard, has been granted in

custody to a family friend." The judge looked at me kindly. I glanced at Mrs. Thompkins next to me, thinking how strange it would be to go home to her house, right next door to my old life, to sleep in her guest room for the next four months until I turned eighteen.

If I had a boyfriend, I could move in with him. So I guessed breaking up with Chad Woolcott right before I went to Europe had been premature. I sighed, but the sigh turned into a sob, and I choked it back.

The judge began talking about probate and executors, and my mind got fuzzy.

I loved Bridget Thompkins—she'd been the grandmother I'd never had. When her husband had died three years ago, it was like losing a grandfather. Could I stay in my own house and just have her be my guardian, next door?

"And is the person named Axel Govin in the courtroom?" Judge Dailey asked, looking over her glasses.

"*Axelle Gau-vanh*," a voice behind me said, giving the name a crisp French pronunciation.

"Axelle Gauvin," the judge repeated patiently.

Mrs. Thompkins and I frowned at each other.

"Ms. Gauvin, Michel Allard's will clearly states that he wished you to become the guardian of his only minor child, Thais Allard. Is this your understanding?"

I blinked rapidly. *Whaaat?*

"Yes, it is, Your Honor," said the voice behind me, and I whirled around. Axelle Gauvin, whom I'd never heard of in my life, looked like the head dominatrix of

9

an expensive bordello. She had shining black hair cut in a perfect, swingy bell right above her shoulders. Black bangs framed black, heavily made-up eyes. Bright blood-red lips either pouted naturally or had been injected with collagen. The rest of her was a blur of shining black leather and silver buckles. In summer. Welsford, Connecticut, had never seen anything like this.

"Who is that?" Mrs. Thompkins whispered in shock.

I shook my head helplessly, trying to swallow with an impossibly dry throat.

"Michel and I hadn't seen each other recently," the woman said in a sultry, smoker's voice, "but we'd always promised each other I'd take care of little Thais if anything happened to him. I just never thought it would." Her voice broke, and I turned around to see her dabbing at eyes as dark as a well.

She'd said my name correctly—even the judge had pronounced it Thay-iss, but Axelle had known it was Tye-ees. Had she known my dad? How? My whole life, it had been me and my dad. I'd known he'd dated, but I'd always met the women. None of them had been Axelle Gauvin.

"Your Honor, I—" Mrs. Thompkins began, upset.

"I'm sorry," the judge said gently. "You're still the executor for all Mr. Allard's personal possessions, but the will clearly states that Ms. Axelle Gauvin is to assume custody of the minor. Of course, you could challenge the will in court . . . but it would be an expensive and lengthy process." The judge took off her glasses, and the icy knowledge that this was real, that I really might end up with this hard-looking stranger in back of me, began to filter into my panicked mind. "Thais will be eighteen in only four months, and at that time she'll be legally free to decide where she wants to live and with whom. Although I would hope that Ms. Gauvin is sensitive to the fact that Thais is about to start her senior year of high school and that it would be least disruptive if she could simply stay in Welsford to do so."

"I know," said the woman, sounding regretful. "But sadly, my home is in New Orleans, and my business precludes my being able to relocate here for the next year. Thais will be coming to New Orleans with me."

I sagged down on my bed, feeling my somewhat threadbare quilt under my fingers. I felt numb. I was embracing numbness. If I ever let myself not feel numb, a huge, howling pain would tear up from my gut and burst out into the world in a shrieking, unstoppable, hysterical hurricane.

I was going to New Orleans, Louisiana, with a leather-happy stranger. I hated to even speculate on how she knew my dad. If they'd had any kind of romantic relationship, it would take away the dad I knew and replace him with some brain-damaged unknown. She'd said they'd been friends. Such good friends that he'd given her his only child, yet had never mentioned her name to me once.

A tap on my door. I looked up blankly as Mrs.

11

Thompkins came in, her gentle, plump face drawn and sad. She carried a sandwich and a glass of lemonade on a tray, which she set on my desk. She stood by me, brushing her fingers over my hair.

"Do you need any help, dear?" she whispered.

I shook my head and tried to manage a brave smile, which failed miserably. Inside me a hollow wail of pain threatened to break through. It hit me over and over again, yet I still couldn't quite take it in. My dad was dead. Gone forever. It was literally unbelievable.

"You and I know everything we want to say," Mrs. Thompkins went on in a soft voice. "Saying it just seems too hard right now. But I'll tell you this: it's just for four months. If it works out and you want to stay down there"—she made it sound like hell—"then that's fine, and I'll wish you well. But if you want to come back after four months, I'll be here, with open arms. Do you understand?"

I nodded and did smile then, and she smiled back at me and left.

I couldn't eat. I didn't know what to pack. What had happened to my life? I was about to leave everything and everyone I had ever known. I'd been looking forward to going away to college next year—had imagined leaving this place, this room. But I wasn't ready now, a year early. I wasn't ready for any of this.

Connected by Fate

I reach out through the darkness
To touch the ones I need
I send my spirit with a message
It finds their spirits where they reside
We are connected by time
We are connected by fate
We are connected by life
We are connected by death
Go.

In this still room, the candle flame barely wavered. How lucky, truly, for them to find such a suitable place. Daedalus liked this little room, with its attic ceiling sloping sharply downward toward the walls. He sat comfortably on the wooden floor, nailed into place over two hundred years before. Breathing slowly, he watched the candle flame shine unwaveringly, upside down in the faintly amethyst-colored glass, as if the ball itself were a large eye peering out into the world.

"Sophie," Daedalus breathed, imagining her the way she'd looked when he'd seen her last. What, ten years ago? More. *Sophie. Feel my connection, hear my message.*

Daedalus closed his eyes, scarcely breathing, sending thoughts across continents, across time itself.

Cherche nouveau: L'histoire de France. Sophie tapped the words out on her keyboard, enjoying the instant gratification, the enormous well of knowledge at her fingertips. With every passing age, things became more wondrous. Yes, there were downsides to progress. There were many, many things she missed. But each new day revealed a new wonder also.

"*Veux-tu le saumon?*" Manon asked, the phone pressed against her ear. "*Pour dîner,*" she clarified when Sophie looked at her.

Sophie nodded. She didn't care what she ate. She couldn't understand Manon's various hungers: food, drink, cigarettes, people. Sophie thirsted for knowledge, for learning. One day, somehow, if she could fill her brain with enough truth and understanding—then perhaps she could begin to understand herself, her life, the lives that were irrevocably entwined with hers. Maybe.

A thin tendril of cigarette smoke floated over to her. Manon was still walking around, phone pressed against her ear, ordering food from the concierge.

The results of Sophie's search filled her laptop screen, and she leaned forward. At that moment, with no warning, the words wavered, as if underwater. Sophie frowned, glancing at the floor to make sure the surge protector was active. This computer was practically brand-new. What—?

14

Sophie, my love. Come to New Orleans. It's important. Daedalus.

The words resolved themselves on Sophie's screen as she watched them, taking them in. Manon hung up the phone and came to see what Sophie was staring at.

"We haven't heard from him in a while," Manon said unnecessarily.

Sophie said nothing.

"Are we going to go?" Manon asked.

Again Sophie didn't reply. Her large brown eyes searched the room, the air, seeming to stare across thousands of miles, straight at Daedalus.

"And now Ouida," Daedalus murmured, clearing his mind of all thought, all feeling. He existed but was unaware of his own being. He was one with the wood, the air, the glass, the flame. . . .

Okay, assuming this sample wasn't contaminated, she could isolate about thirty cells, put them through trypsin-Giemsa staining, and have a nice set of chromosomes to examine. Ouida Jeffers carefully maneuvered the dish containing the genetic material out of the centrifuge. She heard the lab door swing open and shut but didn't look up until the sample was securely on a shelf and the fridge door closed. Not after what had happened last Tuesday. A month's worth of work literally down the drain. God.

"Excuse me, Doctor."

15

Ouida looked over to see her assistant holding out a pink telephone message.

"This came for you."

"Okay, thanks, Scott." Ouida took the message. Maybe it was about that intern she'd interviewed.

Come to New Orleans, Ouida, it said. The hairs on the back of her neck stood up. Breathing quickly, she glanced around the lab, her lab, so familiar, representing everything she'd worked so hard for. *We need you,* said the message. *At last. Daedalus.*

Swallowing, Ouida sank down on a lab stool and reread the message. Relax, calm down. You don't have to go. She looked through the window, honeycombed with wire for security. Outside the sky was clear and blue. New Orleans. New Orleans would be very hot right now.

As soon as he saw Claire, Daedalus grimaced. Clearly she hadn't made huge leaps forward since the last time they'd met. He saw her sprawled gracelessly in a cheap wooden chair. Two uneven rows of upside-down shot glasses gleamed stickily on the Formica table where she rested her elbows.

Claire.

The crowd chanted around her. A beefy, middle-aged man, some sort of Asian, Daedalus couldn't tell which, seemed to rally himself. He tossed back another jolt of whatever white-lightning alcohol they were drinking. Beyond feeling the stinging burn at the back of his throat, he wiped his mouth on his work-shirt sleeve. Dark, half-closed eyes strained to focus on his opponent.

Claire's attention was caught momentarily by the insistent ringing of the bar's wall phone.

Answer it, Claire. Ask not for whom the phone rings; it rings for thee. . . .

The ringing was blinked away as if it were an annoying insect. Claire smiled, and the crowd cheered at this show of bravado. Someone thunked down another heavy shot glass; an unmarked bottle tilted and splashed more rotgut, filling the glass and dousing the table around it.

The crowd started clapping in unison, shouting something. Her name? Some Asian word that meant "crazy white lady"? Daedalus couldn't tell. She wasn't going to answer the phone—no one was. She wouldn't hear his message. He would have to try to catch her when she was more sober. Good luck. It would take her days, at least, to dry out from today's little episode.

Her eyes glowing greenly, as if lit from within, Claire's unsteady hand reached out for the glass. It wobbled, clear liquid running over her fingers. She didn't notice. She held the shot glass to her lips and tossed back her head. Then, triumphantly, she slammed it down on the table. The crowd roared its approval; money openly changed hands. Across from her, the Asian man bluffed by reaching out his hand

17

for another glass but then slowly leaned sideways, sliding gently against the table. He was lying on the floor, eyes shut, shirt wet, before anyone had realized he was out.

Daedalus groaned. All right, later for her.

At least Marcel wasn't likely to be pickling himself from the inside out, Daedalus thought, closing his eyes and focusing on the man who'd been a mystery for as long as Daedalus had known him. *Marcel.* He pictured the youthful face, the smooth, fair skin, the blue eyes, the pale auburn hair.

The candlelight's reflection didn't move while Daedalus gazed at it. *Marcel.*

Daedalus could practically feel the chill wafting off the stone walls in his vision. He mused that he could be seeing Marcel today, a hundred years ago, three hundred years ago, and it would all look the same: the rough stone monastery walls, the dim light, the orderly rows of desks. Three hundred years ago, every desk would have been occupied. But today few Irish families committed younger sons to God so they'd have one less mouth to feed. As a result, only two other occupants kept Marcel silent company in the large hall.

Marcel was hunched over a large book: an original, hand-illuminated manuscript. The gold leaf had faded hardly at all since the time it was ever so carefully pressed in place by a penitent servant of the Holy Mother Church.

Daedalus sent his message, smiling at his own creativity, proud of his strength. Marcel could deny what he was; Daedalus never would. Ouida could ignore her powers, the same powers that Daedalus reveled in daily. Sophie could fill her time with learning and other intellectual pursuits. Daedalus spent his time harvesting strength.

Which was why he was greater than they; why he was the sender and they the receivers.

In the monastery, Marcel's thin shoulders hunched over his manuscript. The beauty of the art in the margins was filling his soul with a too-pleasurable torment—was it a sin to feel such human joy upon seeing the work of men before him? Or had their hands been divinely guided, their illuminations divinely inspired? In which case Marcel was only paying homage to their God by his admiration.

His lips barely moved as he read the Latin words. But—he frowned. He blinked and rubbed a rough sleeve over his eyes. The letters were moving. . . . *Oh no.*

Panicked, Marcel looked up. No one was paying attention. He shielded the book with his body, keeping it out of sight. He would never escape. And never was such a long time. Now he accepted that the fine-edged black letters had rearranged themselves. He read the newly formed words. *Urgent. Come to New Orleans at once. Daedalus.*

Marcel brushed his rough sleeve across the cold sweat dampening his brow. Then he sat, struggling to feel nothing, as he waited for the words to disappear, to become again a prayer in Latin, lauding God. He had to wait a long time.

The last storm had stirred the waters so that fishing or crabbing was pointless. Better to wait till the water cleared, a week, maybe two. Besides clouding the waters with silt, the storm had littered the sandy beaches with all manner of driftwood, dead fish, an empty turtle shell, uglier human detritus: a bicycle tire, someone's bra. There was a story about *that*, Richard bet.

He wanted a smoke, but last time he'd lit up, four different people had given him hell. Whether it was because he looked so young, despite the pierced nose, pierced eyebrow, and visible tattoos, or because they were just worried about this part of the world being polluted, he didn't know.

Might as well give up for now. Go back home, sleep, whatever.

An unexpected tug on his line caught Richard by surprise, and he almost dropped his pole. But his fingers tightened automatically and he quickly turned his reel. He hoped it wasn't a catfish. They were a bitch to get off the line, and ones this big weren't good eating. The flash of sun on silver told him it was something else.

The reel whirred while he pulled. Long, slender body, shiny silver, with spots. Spanish mackerel. Under the length limit—it would have to go back. Richard pulled the line closer, running his fingers down the wet line to unhook the fish.

Its mouth opened. "Richard," the fish croaked. *Ree-shard*.

Richard blinked and then started to grin. He glanced around—unlikely that anyone else could hear his talking fish. He laughed. What a funny idea! A talking fish! This was hysterical.

"Richard," the fish said again. "Come back to New Orleans. It'll be worth your while, I promise. Daedalus."

Richard waited a moment, but the fish had exhausted its message, apparently. Quickly he slipped his fingers down the hook, flipped the fish off it. It dropped the eight feet to the cloudy olive-drab water, its flanks flashing.

Hmm, New Orleans. It hadn't been that long since he'd been back. But long enough. He grinned. A road trip. Just what he needed to cheer himself up.

Daedalus laughed softly to himself, watching Richard gather his gear. It would be good to see him again. Probably.

A sound downstairs drew Daedalus's attention. Moving deliberately, not quickly, he doused his candle and put his glass globe in the cupboard, draping a square of black silk over it. He smudged the circle of salt on the floor, erasing its lines with his foot, then smoothed his hair back.

He felt drained, hungry, thirsty. He'd done a lot in one day—perhaps too much. But there was no time to waste.

21

"Yeah, so she was pissed," Racey reported, flipping her streaked hair back. She leaned against the wall in the tiny curtained dressing cubicle and took a sip of iced coffee.

"Yeah?" I asked absently, unhooking my bra so I could try on a tie-dyed halter top. "What'd she say?"

"She said the next time I missed a circle, my ass would be grass." Racey cocked her head, which made her short, asymmetrical haircut look almost even.

I gave a quick grin—Racey's mom was a riot. More like an older sister than a mom. My grandmother was cool in her own way, but you couldn't get away from the fact that she was a grandmother. True, she was aging well—in fact, her looks hadn't changed much for as long as I could remember. Those were the genes I wanted to inherit—those and Nan's *force de magie.* "And she'd be the lawn mower?" I guessed.

"Yep. Turn around so I can see the back."

"I'm going to look." I pushed open the Indian-bedspread curtain and stepped out to look in the full-length mirror mounted on one wall. I loved Botanika—they always had cool stuff. Food, coffee, tea, witch supplies like candles, oils, crystals. Books, music, incense. A small selection of retro clothes, tie-dyed and batik and funky. Plus it felt so normal here. I'd told Racey about my horrible vision, but only a bit, and I hadn't really told her how freaked I'd been. Even now, days later, I felt a bit weird, like something was about to happen. It was stupid.

Outside, the mirror was cheap and warped, so that I had to stand on my tiptoes to get a good view of the halter. I looked at myself, thinking, *I so lucked out.* Conceited? Well, yeah. But also realistic. Why should I pretend that I didn't enjoy my natural assets? I tugged the shirt up so my silver belly ring showed. Cool.

"Was your grandmother mad?" Racey asked, stirring her coffee with the straw.

"Oh, yeah." I grimaced. "She was burned. I had to vacuum the whole house."

"Poor Cinderella." Racey grinned. "Good thing you have a small house." The contrast of her dark brown hair streaked with white gave her a faintly camouflaged look, like a zebra or a tiger. Her big brown eyes were rimmed in teal today. She'd been my best friend and partner in crime since kindergarten. It helped that her parents and my grandmother belonged to the same coven. The coven we had blown off, the night of the new moon, so we could go bar hopping in the Quarter.

"But it was worth it," I said firmly, checking out my rear view. "I love Amadeo's—full of college guys and tourists. Didn't you have fun?" I smiled, remembering

23

how I hadn't needed to buy myself a single drink—and not because I was working on those guys with spells. It had been just good old-fashioned female charm.

"Yeah, I did, but my magick wasn't worth crap the next day. The alcohol."

"There *is* that," I admitted, deciding to buy the halter. Someday, I'd have to find a way around that annoying truth. I pushed my black hair over my shoulders, then saw how it looked against my skin in back. Excellent. *Thanks, Mom.* Nan had one picture of my mom, and I looked like her: black hair, green eyes, and the weirdest thing of all, we both had a strawberry birthmark in the exact same place. I was still trying to decide if I wanted to get it lasered off—it was on my left cheekbone and looked like, well, frankly, what it looked like depended on how much you'd had to drink. Sometimes a small thistle flower, sometimes an animal footprint (Racey said a very tiny three-toed sloth), sometimes a fleur-de-lis. And my mom, who had died when I was born, had had the same thing. *Quelle bizarre, n'est-ce pas?*

I was heading back into the cubicle when I felt, literally felt, someone's gaze on me. I looked through the few clothing racks out to the main part of the store. And saw him.

My breath stopped in my throat and I froze where I stood. *Déesse.* This was the definition of poleaxed, this stunned feeling, where time stood still and all that crap.

"What?" said Racey, almost bumping into me. She followed my line of vision. "Whoa."

24

The Hottest Guy in the World was staring right at me. I've known my share of hot guys, but this one was in a whole different league. His sable-colored hair was too long, as if he couldn't be bothered to get it cut properly. Dark eyebrows angled sharply over dark eyes. He was young but with strong features, like a man, not a boy. In that instant, I knew we would be together. And I also knew that he wouldn't be easy to wrap around my little finger, like other guys. His open, interested look was a challenge. One that I was going to accept.

I raised my eyebrows slightly, then went slowly into the cubicle, giving him a good look at my back, all bare skin because of the halter. Racey followed me in a second later, and I made an awed, oh-my-God face at her. She shrugged noncommittally.

"You don't think he's too old?" she whispered.

I shook my head and laughed, surprised and a little freaked to notice that my fingers were trembling. Racey helped me undo the back ties, and I scrambled back into my bra. I felt like I'd just run a thousand-meter race, hot and cold and trembly all over.

I was dressed for comfort in an over-dyed man's tank top and a ratty pair of jean shorts that were cut off right below my underwear. While it would have been nice to be wearing something more sophisticated, I knew that most guys would think I looked damn fine.

"That guy is fantastic," I said.

Racey shrugged again. "We don't know him," she pointed out. "He could be anyone."

I looked at her. Racey had never been like this—usually she was as go-get-'em as I was. Did she want him for herself? I didn't think so. She didn't look jealous. Just . . . concerned.

I had to get up my nerve to saunter out of the changing cubicle, the halter in my hand. Which was very unlike me. A guy—any guy—hadn't made me nervous since I was about four years old.

He was still there, not even pretending to be cool or casual. His gaze locked on me like a dark laser, and I felt an actual bona fide shiver go down my spine. Oh my God, this was going to be fun. And scary. Anything that was truly fun always had an element of scary to it.

He didn't smile, or wave, or try to look approachable. Instead, keeping his eyes on me, he nudged a chair out a bit with his foot. *Très* suave.

I was dimly aware of Racey fading into the background like a good best friend. Out of the corner of my eye I saw her settle into a seat at the bar. Then I was at his table, and he pushed the chair out the rest of the way for me. I sat down, dropped the halter on the table, and reached over for his drink. Our eyes stayed locked as I took a sip—he was drinking iced espresso, which seemed impossibly cool. He was perfection. The ultimate. And I was going to show him that we were a matched set.

"I haven't seen you here before," I said, thrilled to hear my voice sound a tiny bit husky, a tiny bit lower than usual. This close, I could see that his eyes were actually an incredibly dark blue, like the sky at midnight. It made him look that much more intense.

"I'm new in town," he said, and *he had a French accent.* God help me.

"How are you liking the local scenery?" I asked, and drank more of his coffee.

He looked at me, and I felt like he was picturing me lying down somewhere with him and he was thinking about what we would do when we got there. My heartbeat sped up.

"I'm liking it," he said, understanding my meaning. He took back his glass and drank from it. "I'm Andre."

I smiled. "Clio."

"Clio," he repeated, and my name with a French accent sounded incredible. I spoke some French, like my grandmother did. Our religion was all based in French from hundreds of years ago. But I didn't have an accent, I mean, except an American one. "Tell me, Clio," he said, leaning toward me over the small table. "Are you what you seem? Would you be dangerous for me to . . . know?"

"Yes. And no," I said steadily, lying through my teeth. I had no idea what I seemed to be, and no way would I tell him that I was dangerous only because I didn't intend to ever let him get away. "What about you?" I asked, feeling like I was walking some fine edge. "Are you dangerous for me to know?"

He smiled then, and I felt my heart shudder to a stop inside my chest. At that moment, I would have given him my hand and let him take me across the world, giving up my home, my grandmother, my friends. "Yes, Clio," he said softly, still smiling. "I'm dangerous for you to know."

I looked back at him, feeling utterly, utterly lost. "Good," I managed, my throat dry.

An instant of surprise crossed his beautiful, sculpted face, and then he actually laughed. He took my hand in both of his. Little sparks of electricity made me tingle all over, and then he turned my hand palm up. He looked at it and slowly traced a finger down the lines in my palm, as if reading my fortune. Then he took out a pen and wrote a phone number on my skin.

"Unfortunately, I'm already late," he said in a voice that was so intimate, so personal, it was as if we were the only two people in Botanika. He stood up—he was tall—and put some money on the table for a tip. "But that's my number, and I'm telling you: if you don't call me, I'll come find you."

"We'll see, won't we?" I said coolly, though inside I was doing an ecstatic victory dance. Something in his eyes flared, making me take a shallow breath, and then it was gone, leaving me to wonder if I had imagined it.

"Yes," he said, sounding deceptively mild. "We will." Turning, he walked with long, easy strides to the door and pushed it open. I watched him pass the plate glass window and had to struggle with myself not to jump up, run after him, and tackle him right there.

Racey slid into the seat opposite mine. "Well?" she said. "What was he like? Did he seem okay?"

28

I let out a deep breath I hadn't realized I'd been holding. "More than okay." I uncurled my fingers, showing Racey his number written on my palm.

Racey looked at me, unusually solemn.

"What?" I asked her. "I've never seen you like this."

"Yeah," she said, and looked away. "I don't know what it is. Usually, you know, we see a guy, and bam, we know what the deal is, how to handle him—no surprises, you know? They're all kind of the same. But this one—I don't know," she said again. "I mean, I just got a funny feeling from him."

"You and me both," I said sincerely, looking at his phone number in my palm.

"It was like I instantly knew he was ... really different," Racey persisted.

I looked at her, interested. She was one of the strongest witches our age in the coven, and besides that, she was my best friend. I totally trusted her.

"Different bad?" I asked. "I didn't see that. He totally knocked me off my feet, but it all felt good." Besides the scary stuff, I meant.

Racey shrugged, as if shaking off bad feelings. "I don't know what I'm doing," she said. "Don't listen to me. He *is* really hot. And I didn't even talk to him." Then she looked at me again. "Just ... be careful."

"Yeah, of course," I said, having no idea what that meant. We got up, and I paid for my new halter, which I planned to wear the next time I saw Andre.

Thais

Okay, one good thing—
beignets—weighed against the katrillion bad things.
Mostly, one incredibly bad thing—not having Dad, who
had been there every day of my life, let me win at
Monopoly, taught me to drive. He'd held me when I
cried, and my eyes filled up now just thinking about it.
He'd been quietly funny, gentle, maybe a little bit distant,
but I'd always known he'd loved me. And I hoped he'd
known how much I loved him.

I swallowed hard and moved on to all the other horrible things: Axelle, the rest of New Orleans, my entire
life, Axelle's creepy friends, being an orphan, my life, the
heat, the bugs, the ridiculous humidity that felt like a
damp fist punching your head when you stepped outside, my life, missing my dad, missing Welsford, missing
Mrs. Thompkins, Axelle, not having a car, being seventeen and starting a new school for senior year, oh yeah,
my *life*, the noise, the crowds, the clogging throngs of
tourists everywhere, drunk and sun-baked by two in the
afternoon because New Orleans is the devil's play-
ground, Axelle, oh, and did I mention going crazy missing my dad?

But the beignets and coffee were unbelievable. Nothing like light, airy, puffs of dough deep-fried in lard and coated with powdered sugar to pick a girl up. And the coffee—oh God. I'd always hated coffee— didn't even like the smell when Dad made it. But the coffee here was boiled with milk and it was fabulous. I came to Café du Monde every day for my caffeine-'n'-cholesterol fix. Another couple of weeks and I would be permanently hyped up and weigh two hundred pounds. The sad thing was, that wouldn't even make my life any worse. I was already at rock bottom. And now I was crying again, dripping tears onto the powdered sugar, as I did almost every time I came here. I pulled more napkins out of the dispenser and wiped my eyes.

I had no idea how this had happened to me. A month ago I was totally normal in every way, living a totally normal life with my totally normal dad. Now, barely four weeks later, I was living with a strange woman (I mean literally strange, as in *bizarre*, not just *unknown*) who had zero idea of what guardianship was all about. She'd told me that she and my dad had had a deep and meaningful friendship but had sometimes lost touch with each other through the years. I was way, way thankful that apparently they'd never actually dated.

Still, Dad must have been out of his gourd to think for even one second that my living with Axelle would be anything close to a good idea. I'd lost track of how many times a day I prayed for this to be a nightmare so I could wake up.

I got up and walked across the street, through Jackson Square. Axelle lived in the French Quarter, the oldest part of New Orleans. I had to admit, it was pretty. The buildings looked European, not southern or colonial, and there was an old-fashioned grace and time-lessness to the place that even I in my misery could appreciate. On the other hand, it was incredibly dirty almost everywhere, and some streets were touristy in a horrible, seedy kind of way. Like all the strip joints on Bourbon Street. Yep, just blocks of strip joints and bars, all being peered into by anyone passing by, even if the person passing by was a *child*.

But there were other streets, not touristy, quiet and serene in a timeless way. Even Welsford was founded only in about 1860. New Orleans had had some sort of settlement here for about 150 years before that. Through hours and hours of walking aimlessly, I had realized that there was a whole separate Quarter that most people never see: the private gardens, hidden courtyards, pockets of lush green almost pulsing with life.

Yet even in the midst of ageless beauty, there was an undercurrent of . . . what? Danger? Not as strong as danger. Not as strong as dread. But like, when I walked under a balcony, I expected a safe to fall on my head. If the same person walked behind me for more than a block, I got nervous. There was a lot of crime here, but my nervousness wasn't even that based in reality. It was more like . . . I expected the sun to never shine again in my life. Or like I had driven into a train tunnel, and there was no end in sight, and a train was coming at me. It was weird, but maybe it was natural to feel that way after everything I had been through.

I turned left and cut down a narrow, one-block-long little street. I waded through a busload of tourists on a walking tour and turned another corner. Two blocks down this street was where I was sentenced to live, at least for the next few months.

Axelle's apartment had once been part of an incredible private home. There was a side gate made of wrought iron, which I unlocked. It led to a narrow, covered driveway, wide enough for carriages, not cars. My feet made faint echoing noises on the cool flagstones, worn from hundreds of years of use. The front door was in the back of the house. Four buildings bordered a private courtyard, which had a weensy swimming pool and lushly overgrown plant beds around the walls.

Sighing, feeling like an anvil was on my chest, I turned my key in the lock. With any luck Axelle wouldn't be here—she'd already be out for the evening, and I wouldn't have to go. Last night she'd brought me to three different bars, despite my reminding her that not only was I not twenty-one, but I wasn't even eighteen yet. At all three places, the bouncer or doorman had looked at me, opened his mouth as if to card me, which I was hoping for, because then I could go home and go to bed—but then they'd just shut their mouths and let me pass. I guessed Axelle knew them, and they'd let her do whatever.

I pushed open the door, to be met by a blessed whoosh of air-conditioning, and found I was out of luck. Axelle lounged on her black leather sofa, her clothes making slight sibilant noises when she shifted. She was smoking and talking on the phone and barely looked up at me when I came in.

To add to my fun, her creepy friends Jules and Daedalus were there too. I'd met them practically the moment we got off the plane in New Orleans. Neither of them was her boyfriend, but they were around a lot. Jules was good-looking in a Denzel Washington kind of way, poised and put together, and seemed about Axelle's age, early thirties. Daedalus was old enough to be her father, like in his mid-fifties. He reminded me of a used car salesman, always smiling but the smile never reaching his eyes.

"Ah! Thais," said Daedalus, looking up from a thick book. Jules also looked up and smiled, then continued examining a map on the small round dining table at one end of the huge main room. At the other end were a fireplace and sitting area. The tiny kitchen was open to the big room, separated by a black granite counter. Axelle's bedroom and huge, pathologically crowded and messy closet were down a short hallway. My tiny bedroom, which was essentially a former lean-to tacked onto the main house as an outdoor kitchen, opened off the back of the kitchen.

"Hi," I said, heading for privacy.

"Wait, Thais," Jules said. He had a beautiful deep

voice. "I'd like you to meet our friend Richard Landry." He gestured toward the main room, and someone I hadn't noticed stepped through the haze of Axelle's cigarette smoke.

"Hey," he said.

I blinked. At first glance he appeared to be my age, but in the next second I realized he was actually younger—maybe fourteen? He was a bit taller than me and had warm brown hair, streaked from the sun, and brown eyes. I couldn't help standing still for a moment to take him in: he was the only fourteen-year-old I'd ever seen with a silver stud through his eyebrow, a silver ring through one nostril, and tattoos. He was wearing a black T-shirt with the sleeves torn off and long black jeans despite the heat.

I realized I was staring and tried to recover. "Hi, Richard," I said, pronouncing it the way Jules had: Reeshard. He just nodded, looking at me in a weirdly adult way, like: appraising. Yes, he won the weirdest-kid-I'd-ever-met award. And why on earth was he hanging out with these people? Maybe his parents were friends of theirs?

Axelle hung up the phone and got to her feet. Today, in deference to the ninety-eight-degree weather, she was wearing a black, satiny cat suit. "Oh, good, you met Richard," she said. "Well, you all ready?"

Jules, Daedalus, and Richard nodded, and Richard put down his glass.

"We won't be long," said Axelle, unlocking a door

that I hadn't even seen the first four days I was here. It was built into the deep molding of the main room, a hidden door. I'd almost jumped out of my skin one day when I'd thought I was alone and then suddenly Daedalus had appeared out of the wall. Now that I knew it was there, I could easily see its outlines and the round brass lock. It led to stairs, I knew that much, but I wasn't allowed in—it was always locked when Axelle wasn't home.

I watched silently as the three guys followed Axelle.

I was convinced they did drugs up there. And now they were dragging a kid into their web. True, a strange, hard-core kid, but still. The door clicked shut with a heavy finality, and I prowled restlessly around the main room, wondering if I should do something. Okay, for the three weird adults, that was one thing. They might be complete dope fiends, but they'd never hit me or come on to me or anything. But now they were corrupting a kid—if there was anything left in Richard to corrupt. That was definitely wrong.

Unsure what to do with my concern, I wandered around, picking up used glasses and loading them into the dishwasher. Axelle was the world's biggest slob, and I'd started tidying up out of self-defense, just so I'd have clean plates to eat off of, etc.

"Mreow?" Minou, Axelle's cat, jumped up on the kitchen counter. I scratched him absently behind the ears and then refilled his food bowl. Like the hidden door, Minou had shown up several days after I got here, but Axelle knew him and actually had cat food, so I figured he was hers. Guess what color he was.

I gathered a stack of newspapers, and the weird domesticness of the situation suddenly hit me. I blinked back tears, remembering how I'd done the same kind of stuff at home, with Dad, and how I'd grumbled about it and made him remind me five times and stuff. Now, what I wouldn't give to be at home with Dad nagging me! I would be the perfect daughter if I could only have another chance. I gulped, thinking maybe it was time to go cry on my bed for a while.

"Excuse me."

I whirled, sniffing and brushing my hand across my eyes. I hadn't heard Richard come up behind me. I closed the dishwasher door. "What?" I said, feeling unnerved.

"Axelle sent me down for matches," he explained in a husky, un-kid-like voice, stepping past me into the narrow kitchen. He was slender but wiry, with defined muscles. He was wearing black motorcycle boots.

"Don't you—?" I began, and he glanced up at me. I could see that even though he was young, he would probably be really good-looking when he grew up. If he lost the face jewelry. "Don't you think you're a little young for that?" I waved my hand toward the hidden stairway. Richard looked at me, expressionless. "I mean—do your folks know where you are? Don't you worry about getting in trouble or having it lead to bigger stuff that could actually really be dangerous?"

Richard picked up the box of matches. "I'm an orphan, honey," he said, with a funny little smile. "And it's not what you think, upstairs. You'll find out."

Uh-oh. That didn't sound good. "I mean, it's not too late to quit," I said, feeling more and more unsure.

He did smile then, showing a hint of the man he would become in a couple of years. "It's way too late to quit," he said, and gave a little laugh, like there was a private joke somewhere. He left me and went back through the door, and feeling completely weirded out, I glanced absently at the stack of newspapers.

Time to register for school, those attending Orleans Parish public schools, I read. I had to move Minou's tail to finish the headline. School started on August 26, barely three weeks away. It listed a web site where you could register online.

"Oh, Thais," said Axelle, coming into the kitchen. She rummaged in the cupboards and pulled out a box of salt. "Listen, don't go anywhere—we'll be done in a while and then we're going out to dinner."

I nodded. We always went out to dinner. "Um, I have to register for school."

Axelle looked at me blankly.

I tapped the paper. "It says it's time to register if you're going to public school. Which I assume I am."

She seemed to recover and said, "Well, you don't have to go if you don't want. You've probably gone enough, right?"

Now I stared at her, her beautiful face that never

seemed to show lack of sleep or hangovers or anything else, the black eyes that had no pupils. "I haven't graduated high school," I said slowly, as if I were explaining something to a child. "I have one more year."

"Well, what's one year?" she asked, shrugging. "I bet you know everything you need to know. Why don't you just hang out, relax?"

My mouth dropped open. "If I don't graduate high school, I won't be able to go to college."

"You mean you'd sign up for four more years?" She looked appalled.

"How am I going to get a *job?*" Or did I not need one, here on Planet Unreality?

Now she looked downright shocked. "*Job?*"

Okay. I was getting nowhere. I could see that. *Thanks, Dad,* I thought, tasting bitterness in the back of my throat. *You sure can pick 'em.* I took a deep breath and let it out. "I'll take care of it," I said calmly. "I'm going to school, and I'll register myself. I'll let you know what happens."

Axelle looked like she was trying to think up a good argument but couldn't come up with anything. "Well, if that's what you want to do," she said reluctantly.

"Yes," I said firmly. "Don't worry about it."

"Okay." She sighed heavily, as if she couldn't believe Michel Allard's child could be so incredibly unreasonable. I picked up the newspaper and headed back into my room, where I carefully shut the door. Then I lay down on my bed, put a pillow over my face, and howled.

So Much Has Changed

"*C'est impossible*," Daedalus muttered in disgust. He banged his fist down on the hood of the car. "*C'est impossible!*"

"Hey!" said Axelle. "*La voiture, c'est à moi!*" She carefully examined the hood of her pink Cadillac.

Daedalus folded his arms across his chest and joined Richard and Jules, who were leaning against the side of Axelle's car, staring across the street. Axelle lit a cigarette.

Jules made a face. "Must you smoke even here?"

"Yes," Axelle said evenly. "Are you going to lecture me about the health disadvantages?"

Richard chuckled, and Jules looked away.

"It's unpleasant is all," he said.

"Then stand *downwind*," said Axelle.

"Stop it, you two," said Daedalus. "We can't start arguing among ourselves. Now, more than ever, we have to stand together."

"Has Sophie come yet?" Axelle asked.

"I think she and Manon are coming tomorrow," said Daedalus. He let out a breath and looked across the street, still unbelieving. "This *is* the place?" he asked for the fifth time.

"It's the place," Jules said dispiritedly. "It has to be."

The four of them stood in a line against the car. Across the street, where they had expected to find thick woods and swamps as far as the eye could see, there was instead a huge Wal-Mart Supercenter. And a huge parking lot. And other stores in a line next to it.

"When's the last time anyone was here?" Daedalus asked.

They thought, shrugged.

"Long time," Axelle said at last. "Obviously."

"Hang on." Richard leaned into the open window of the car and pulled out their old map. He took the recent map from Daedalus and spread them both out on the hood of the car. "Okay, here's New Orleans," he said, pointing to the city within the crescent bend of the river. "And this is about where we are." He traced a slender finger down a blue highway line, south-southwest of New Orleans.

"They're two completely different maps," said Axelle.

Daedalus saw what she meant. "What's the date on that first map?"

"Uh, 1843," Richard said, finding the date in one corner.

"And this is a current map," Daedalus clarified. "Clearly, the older map is wildly inaccurate—it's not a satellite-data topographical map. The same features don't even appear on both. Look, Lac Méchant, Lac Penchant. This one is called Grand Barataria, and now it's called, uh, Lake Salvador. I think." He squinted at the two maps, then glanced up and saw that this afternoon's quick, heavy thunderstorm was on its way.

"Crap," Axelle said.

"But this is the map we always used," Jules said.

"But it's been a long time," Richard pointed out. "Even the actual courses of the rivers have changed. The coastline has changed a lot. With every hurricane that's hit Louisiana, some aspect of the landscape *changed*."

"Now what?" Jules asked, frustration in his voice. "This is a major point."

"Yes, Jules, we *know*," Daedalus said, hearing himself sound testy. He tried to dampen his irritation. They needed to pull together, to work as one. He reached out and put a hand on Jules's shoulder. "I'm sorry, old friend. I'm upset. But this is only a temporary setback, I'm sure. We'll do more research. We'll look at maps from different years and compare them. It will show us how the landmarks have changed. From that we can extrapolate where we need to be looking. It will take time, but we can do it."

"We only have a little time," Jules said.

Again Daedalus squelched his temper. "We have time enough," he said, trying to sound both certain and reassuring. "We'll get started tonight." He looked over at Richard, who'd been quiet. That handsome child's face, those old, old eyes. Richard met his gaze and nodded. Daedalus got into the car just as the first big raindrops hit the windshield. They had to pull this off. This was their only chance. Who knew if they would ever have another?

Half an hour late. That seemed about right. If he was still here, he was serious and had staying power; if he was gone, then good riddance.

(Actually, if he was gone, I would track him down like a dog.)

We were supposed to meet at Amadeo's at nine. It was nine thirty, and the place was starting to fill up. I looked at the bouncer when I went in, and he automatically started to card me.

You don't want to do that, I thought, sending him a quick distraction spell. Just then, something at the back of the bar caught his eye, and he turned, striding through the crowd like a bull through a field of wheat.

I slipped inside and smiled as I saw some regulars. I could feel admiring looks from people and hoped Andre appreciated the skintight white jeans and tie-dyed halter. I flipped my hair back, looking unconcerned, and slowly examined the patrons.

I felt him before I saw him. All of a sudden, my skin tingled, as if someone had shocked me with static. The next moment, a warm hand was on my bare back, and when I turned, I was practically in his arms.

"You're late," he said, looking into my eyes until I felt breathless.

"I'm here now."

"Yes. What do you want to drink?" Expertly he wove us through the crowd until we could stand at the bar to order. Nothing too crass or too childish. "A margarita," I said. "No salt."

Five minutes later we had made our way into Amadeo's back room, where a small stage filled one end. Sometimes on weekends they had live bands, but it was a weeknight, and instead people were clustered around small tables and clumped onto the easy chairs and small couches scattered around the room. It was very dark, and the walls were covered with flocked red wallpaper so kitschy it was in again.

Andre led me to a battered purple love seat that was already occupied by a couple of college guys. He didn't say anything, just stood there, but somehow they suddenly got the urge to get refills on their drafts.

I sank down first, taking Andre's hand and pulling him down next me. He smiled slightly and didn't resist; then he was on the love seat and with no hesitation kept coming at me until our mouths were touching, our eyes wide open. I held my right hand still over the back of the love seat so I wouldn't spill my drink, but the rest of me leaned against Andre, wanting to sink into him, eat him up, melt our bodies together.

Minutes later one of us pulled back—I don't know who. I took a sip of my drink, feeling stunned and hot and nervous and very, very turned on. I glanced uncertainly at him, and he looked like everything I felt.

"What do you have?" I asked, nodding toward his drink.

"Seven-Up," he said, fishing the maraschino cherry out with long, graceful fingers. He held it out to me and I went for it, loving the burst of candied oversweetness in my mouth. When I could talk, I said, "Oh, sure, get the girl drunk while you stay totally in control." Which, to tell you the truth, did not seem like a good situation for me to be in. I mean, I was practically blind with lust for Andre, but I still had one or possibly two wits about me.

Andre gave me a crooked smile and I silenced an involuntary whimper. "Number one," he said softly in his accented voice, "I don't think you would need to be drunk, and number two, I'm not drinking, but somehow I feel I've lost control anyway."

Okay, I was in love. And this is how sappy it was: I was totally, completely, one hundred percent happy and content to be sitting on that lumpy love seat in that crowded bar, drinking my drink and just staring into his dark blue eyes. I wanted for nothing, needed nothing, had to go nowhere. I could sit there and feast my eyes on him till the end of time.

I looked at him thoughtfully, running one finger around the edge of my glass. "No, I wouldn't have to be drunk," I agreed shakily. I leaned back against the side of the love seat and stretched my legs across his lap. My bare feet felt the warmth of his hard thigh through his black jeans, and I pressed them down experimentally. He had muscles.

"'Tell me about yourself,'" I said, pushing my hair back. I played with the straw in my glass and smiled. "Where have you been all my life?"

He smiled too, getting the corny reference. Despite everything, I remembered how Racey had felt about him, and I owed it to her—and to myself—to find out a little bit about him before, say, we got married.

"Andre what?" I prompted, when he didn't answer. "Are you still in school? Where do you live?"

"Andre Martin," he said, giving his last name the French pronunciation: Mar-taihn. I blinked. "I'm taking a year off, out of university, to work for my uncle's law firm here. As a paralegal. I have my own apartment in the Quarter." His warm hands slid under my jeans and massaged my calves. It made my brain feel like mush, or maybe that was because I had drained my large margarita. "Not far from here," he volunteered, smiling wickedly. I put the glass down on the little table next to the love seat.

"Andre Martin?" I said, making sure.

"Yes."

I felt like I'd been looking at his face my whole life. "That's so weird," I said, feeling distinctly fuzzy-headed. "That's my name too. Clio Martin. Isn't that weird?"

He looked amused, then considered it. "Martin is not so unusual a name," he pointed out.

"Yeah, I guess you're right," I said. "It just seemed funny—having the same last name." My head was suddenly very heavy; I dropped it back over the arm of the love seat. Involuntarily I moaned at the strength of Andre's fingers rubbing my legs.

He laughed, then swung my legs over the side again, which pulled me up next to him. He put his arms around me and kissed me.

Things after that were a little blurry. I know he asked me to go home with him, and, miracle of miracles, I said no. I couldn't make it *too* easy for him. I know we kissed and made out and held each other so tightly that at one point my top had his shirt's button impressions on it, which struck us both as really funny.

I know I wanted another margarita and instead received a 7-Up, which made me fall even more in love with him. I could trust him.

And I know that by the time we finally said goodbye, he walked me to my car and made sure I was straight enough to drive, which I truly was—especially since I did a silent dissipation spell as soon as I was behind the wheel. Tonight's alcohol would dampen my abilities tomorrow, but right now the magick sang through my veins. Losing every bit of the margarita's effect was sad, but I also knew if I drove impaired and killed myself, my grandmother would pull me back from the dead so she could kill me all over again.

I rolled down my window, the engine of my battered little Camry humming.

"I had a good time tonight," I said. Major understatement.

He brushed his fingers along my cheek, rubbing his thumb over my birthmark. "So did I," he said seriously, then leaned in the window and kissed me long and hard. "It's okay if I call you?" I had given him my cell phone number.

"Yes," I said, surpassing the first understatement.

"Drive carefully." His look made me feel like we were already joined, one, forever.

I nodded, put the car in gear, and pulled out. He was in my rearview mirror until I turned the corner.

> Seed of life, I nourish you
> I give you room to grow
> I give you friends to grow with
> The sun and rain are all for you
> Your leaves unfurl, your budding show
> To all I am your gardensmith.

I knew better than to roll my eyes or act impatient. Nan always said little spells when she planted things, and of course her garden, the whole yard, was the most perfectly balanced, beautiful garden for blocks. Yet there was a part of me that was thinking, *It's just okra.*

She patted the earth down firmly around the okra

seed, a little smile on her face. She looked perfectly calm, at ease. I was *dying*. It was a thousand degrees outside, and my T-shirt was already damp with sweat. I felt totally gross. At least no one but Nan would see me like this.

Nan looked up at me in that way that felt like she was seeing right through my eyes into the back of my skull. "Not your cup of tea, is it?" she asked with humor.

I showed her my dirty, broken fingernails and the blister beginning on my thumb. She laughed.

"Thank you for your sympathy," I muttered.

"How are you going to be a witch without a garden?" she asked.

"I'll hire someone," I said.

"Will you hire someone to study for you?" she asked, more seriously. "Or maybe you should hire someone to do your drinking for you."

I looked up in alarm. "I haven't been drinking."

She gave me an "oh, come on" face. "Clio—your magick is very strong." She brushed my damp hair off my cheek. "It was strong in your mother also. But she died before she could come into her full power." Her eyes had a faraway, sad look in them. "I want to see *you* come into your full power. Unfortunately, the only way to get there is actually to study, to learn, to practice. The only way to practice meaningfully is to not have dulled your senses. You can be a strong witch or you can be a weak witch. It's up to you."

"It's summertime," I said, hating how whiny and childish I sounded. "I want to have fun."

"All right, have fun," she said. "But you'll be eighteen in November. And I'm telling you now, you're nowhere near ready for your rite of ascension."

Now she had my full and undivided attention. "What? Really? I didn't know it was that bad."

She nodded, looking sad and wise and somehow older than usual. "It's that bad, honey. If you work your butt off, you might be able to pass it. Or you can wait a year, when you turn nineteen."

"Oh, I'm so sure," I sputtered, thinking of all the other kids who'd made their rites of ascension when they were eighteen. No one had *ever* failed and had to wait till they were nineteen. I would never live it down. I would embarrass my grandmother, who everyone considered one of the best teachers. I would look like a total loser, when really, I should be impressing the hell out of everyone. Damn it! All I wanted to do was see Andre. I didn't want to study, didn't want to practice, didn't want to stop ingesting fun things like margaritas.

"It's just that sometimes, studying seems a little, well, boring," I said delicately. "I always feel like I want lightning and sparks and *big* magick, you know?" I held my arms out to the sides to demonstrate "big magick."

Nan looked at me sharply. "Big magick is dangerous magick," she said. "Even if it's for good. Remember, what has a front has a back, and the bigger the front, the bigger the back."

I nodded, thinking, *Whatever the hell that means.* "Okay, I'll try to study more."

Nan stood and brushed her hands off on her old-fashioned apron. "Like I said, it's up to—" She stopped, her words trailing away. She stood very still, her hands frozen, while she looked all around us. Up at the sky, where the usual afternoon storm clouds were gathering, down the street, across the street, at our house and side yard.

"What's the matter?" I stood up also.

Nan looked at me, as if surprised to see me—I mean, really looked at me, like she was actually trying to tell who I was. It was creepy, and I wondered for a second if she'd had a stroke or something.

"What's the matter?" I said. "Nan, are you all right? Let's go into the house—I'll get you some cold lemonade, okay?"

She blinked then and glanced around us once more. "No, I'm all right, honey. It's just—a storm is coming."

"It always comes in the afternoon in the summer," I said, still gently tugging her toward the front steps. "Every day, around three, a storm. But they always blow over fast."

"No," she said. "No." Her voice sounded stronger, more like her. "Not a rainstorm. I mean a bigger storm, one that will . . ." Her words trailed off again, and she looked at the ground, lost in thought.

"A hurricane?" I asked, trying to understand. She was totally creeping me out.

She didn't answer.

Thais

I looked around and sighed. *Great. One of these dreams. Just what I need.*

I'd always had incredibly realistic, Technicolor, all-senses-on dreams my whole life. I'd tried telling Dad about them, but though he was sympathetic, he didn't really get what I was talking about. It wasn't every single night, of course. But maybe 65 percent of the time. In my dreams I felt cold and hot, could smell things, taste things, feel the texture of something in my mouth.

Once, after a shop downtown had been held up, I'd dreamed I'd been in that shop and had gotten shot. I'd felt the burning heat of the bullet as it bored through my chest, felt the impact from the blow knock me off my feet. Tasted the warm blood that rose up in my mouth. Felt myself staring at the shop ceiling, old-fashioned tin, while I slowly lost consciousness, bleeding to death. But it had been just a dream.

The really annoying thing was, even though I almost always knew I was dreaming, I was powerless to stop them. Only a few times I had called, "Cut!" and managed to get myself out of some situation. Mostly I just had to suck it up.

Which explained why I was standing in the middle of this swamp/jungle place, thinking, *Damn it.*

This would teach me to buy touristy postcards to send to my friends back home. At the time I'd thought they were funny—pictures of a Louisiana swamp, or a huge plantation house, or the front of a strip joint on Bourbon Street—all with a tiny picture of myself pasted on them. But apparently the images had sunk into my subconscious too well.

Hence the swamp. *Okay, I need to release any feelings about this place,* I thought, *and just see what happens, what the dream needs to show me.* I looked around. My bare feet were ankle-deep in reddish-green-brownish water, surprisingly warm. Beneath my feet the bottom was superslick clay, fine silt that squished up between my toes. The air was thick and heavy and wet, and my skin was covered with sweat that couldn't evaporate. Hardly any sunlight penetrated to the ground, and I tried to convince myself it was a fascinating example of a rainforestlike habitat.

Then I saw the ghosts. Translucent, gray, Disney World ghosts, floating from one tree to the next, as if playing ghost hide-and-seek. I saw a woman in old-fashioned clothes, a gray-haired man in his Sunday best. There was a hollow-eyed child, wearing rags, eating rice from a bowl with her fingers. And a slave, wrists wrapped in chains, the skin scraped raw and bleeding. I began to feel cold, and all the tiny little hairs all over my body stood on end. There was no sound—no splash of water, no call of bird, no rustle of leaves. Dead silence.

"Okay, I've seen enough," I told myself firmly. "Time to wake up."

The mists around me got thicker, more opaque, swirling in a smoky paisley pattern around the trees, the cypress knees, the Spanish moss. Maybe ten yards away, a log rolled—no, it was an alligator, covered with thick, dark green skin. I saw its small yellow eyes for a moment, right before it silently slid into the water, headed my way.

Crap.

Something touched my bare ankle, and I yelped, jumping a foot in the air. Heart pounding, I looked down. An enormous snake was twining around my bare leg. It was huge, as thick around as my waist, impossibly strong, dark, and wet. Its triangular head framed two cold, reptilian eyes. The constant flick of its tongue across my skin made me feel like I was covered with crawling insects. Adrenaline raced coldly through my veins, tightening my throat, speeding up my heart. I tried to run, but it held me fast. Uselessly I pushed at it with all my strength, trying to uncoil it from around me. I punched its head and barely made it bob. It coiled around me till I was weighted down by snake, surrounded by snake, my breath being squeezed from my lungs. I gasped for breath, trying to scream, digging my fingernails into the heavy, coiled muscles around my neck, and suddenly I knew that I was going to die, here in this swamp, without understanding why.

"*Daddy!*" With my very last shred of strength, a scream burst from my throat. Then it was choked off— the snake was around my neck. I couldn't feel my arms anymore. I was light-headed and couldn't see. . . .

Then all around me the world grew bright, like a floodlight had been turned on. I gasped and blinked wildly, unable to see, the snake still around my neck—

"Hold still, damn it," said a voice, and strong hands worked at my neck. I sucked in a deep breath as the snake's grip loosened and I could breathe again. I gulped in cool, air-conditioned air, feeling the cold sweat run down my temple, down my back.

"Wha, wha—"

"I heard you yell," Axelle said, and with difficulty I brought her into focus.

Slowly I struggled upright, my hand to my throat. I was still gasping, still choked by panic. I looked around. I was in my little room at Axelle's in New Orleans. She looked uncharacteristically disheveled—hair rumpled from sleep, grumpy, her body barely contained inside a red lace slip.

"What happened?" I croaked, my voice as hoarse as if I'd been coughing all night. Looking down, I saw that my top sheet had gotten twisted into a thick rope, and this had been wound around my neck.

"I was having a nightmare," I said, still trying to orient myself. "A snake . . ." I pushed the sheet away, kicking it away from me, wiping my hand across my damp forehead. "God."

"I heard you yell," Axelle said again.

"How did you get in? My door was locked."

She shrugged. "It's my apartment. Nothing is locked to me."

Great. "Well, thank you," I said awkwardly. "I thought I was dying—it was . . . really realistic." I swallowed again, my hand brushing my throat, which ached.

Axelle frowned and nudged my fingers away, tilting my chin. She looked at my neck, at the sheet, and back at my neck. At the expression on her face, I got up and shakily made my way to the little mirror over the white bamboo dresser. My neck was bruised, scraped, as if I truly had been strangled.

My eyes widened. Axelle went to my window and ran her hands around the edge of it. The shutters were pulled and bolted from inside, and the window had been locked.

"It was just a dream," I said faintly. Unless of course Axelle had been trying to kill me. But I didn't sense danger from her—she'd just woken me up. It sounded stupid—it was hard to explain. But sometimes I had a sense about people—like in seventh grade, when I had instantly hated Coach Deakin, even though everyone else had loved him and thought he was so great. I'd hated him immediately, for no reason. And then six months later he had been arrested for sexually harassing four students.

I went to the bathroom and splashed water on my face, then drank some, feeling the ache in my throat as it went down.

"I don't see how you could do that to yourself," Axelle murmured as I shook out the covers, untwisting the sheet and spreading everything flat. "You dreamed it was a snake?"

I nodded, folding my covers way down out of the way at the bottom of the bed. I didn't want them anywhere near my head. "In a swamp."

Axelle looked at me thoughtfully, and, for the first time since I'd known her, I saw shrewd intelligence in her black eyes. "Well, leave your door open tonight," she said, pushing it wide. "In case you . . . need anything."

"Okay."

Murmuring to herself, Axelle traced her fingers lightly around my door frame, almost like she was writing a secret message with her fingers.

"What are you doing?"

She shrugged. "Just making sure the door is all right."

O-kaaay.

"Call me if you . . . get scared or anything," Axelle said before she turned to go.

I nodded. And the weird part was: I actually found that *comforting*.

Then she was gone, her red slip swishing lightly through the kitchen.

I sat up in bed, propped against the headboard, and didn't go back to sleep until the sun came through my shutters.

Time Is Running Out

Jules spread his latest acquisition over the worktable in Axelle's attic room.

"What year is that?" Daedalus asked.

Jules checked. "Nineteen-ten."

This was painstaking, often frustrating work, Jules thought. But perhaps they were making slow progress.

"Look," Jules said, tracing a finger down the Atchafalaya River. "It's different here, and here."

Daedalus nodded. "It must have jumped its banks between the time this map was drawn and the one from . . . 1903."

"Let's get a computer up here so we can double-check hurricane dates, floods, things like that," Jules said.

Daedalus gave him that patient-father look he hated. "We can't have a computer up here," he said, just as Jules remembered that electrical appliances wreaked havoc with magickal fields.

"Oh yeah," he said, irritated that he hadn't thought of that. "It's just a pain to run up and down those stairs every time we need to check something. And that girl is on it a lot."

Daedalus glanced at him, keeping his finger on a map. "Is Axelle monitoring her?"

Jules shrugged. "I don't know."

He heard Daedalus sigh as though once again, he himself had to do everything, had to make sure everything was being done right, done his way. Jules clenched his jaw. He was getting fed up with Daedalus's attitude Daedalus wasn't the mayor, after all. They were all equal in the Treize, right? Wasn't that what they had agreed? So why was Daedalus issuing orders—find this, get that, go look up such-and-such? And Jules knew he wasn't the only one whose nerves Daedalus was stepping on.

Richard came in, holding a bottle of beer. Jules tried not to glance at his watch but couldn't help it. And of course Richard saw him.

"Hey, it's five o'clock *somewhere*," he said, popping the top. He took a deep drink, then breathed a contented sigh. "Now *that's* a beer," he said, shaking his hair back. "Thank God for microbreweries. Have you tried this Turbodog?"

"I don't drink," Jules said stiffly, moving to the bookcase and selecting a thick volume with a cracked leather binding.

"It *does* dull your magick, Riche," Daedalus said mildly, still poring over the maps.

"I'll cross that bridge when we come to it," Richard said, seating himself on a stool by the worktable. One knee poked through the huge rip in his jeans. "We don't seem to be close to needing my magick, such as it is."

"It won't be long," Jules said. "We're working on the maps. We're getting the rite into shape, practically everyone is here—we each have a role to perform, and we're doing it." Unconsciously he looked at Daedalus, and the other man met his eyes. Some roles were more challenging than others.

"Practically," Richard said, seizing on the word. "We're missing Claire, Marcel, Ouida, and who else?"

"Ouida's on her way," said Daedalus. "As are Manon and Sophie, I believe. We're still working on Claire and Marcel."

Richard gave a short laugh. "Good luck. So we'll have the map, the rite, the water, the wood—and a full Treize, yes?"

Daedalus straightened and smiled at him. "That's right. This is the closest we've ever come. Nothing will go wrong—we won't let it."

Richard nodded and took another swig from his bottle. Jules didn't look up from the book, pretending to scan the old-fashioned French words. He didn't share Daedalus's optimism. There were too many variables—too many things that could go wrong. And time was running out.

Thais

My life had settled into a routine at Casa Loco: I had somehow become the general houseboy, maid, gofer, and all-around girl Friday. Not that Axelle was forcing me into these roles at gunpoint. Some I did for my own comfort and survival, some out of boredom, and then there were a few things that Axelle asked me to do and I had no good reason not to.

Now that I lived here, there was usually actual food around. The ant problem in the kitchen had been licked, and I could cross the main room in the dark without killing myself. I tried not to think about home or what I would be doing there, but every once in a while I was overwhelmed by longing for my dad and my old life. He used to take me canoeing on the weekends. Or skiing in the winter. Once he'd broken his ankle skiing, and he'd let me decorate his cast, all of it, by myself.

When I got older, my best friend, Caralyn, and I would both get summer jobs at whatever shop in town was hiring. I'd worked at Friendly's Hardware, Marybeth's Ice Cream Shoppe, Joe & Joe's Coffee Emporium, you name it. And after work we'd meet at the pool and go swimming, or hit the movies, or go to the closest mall, twenty miles away.

When I'd mentioned getting a summer job to Axelle, she'd looked at me blankly, as she so often did, and then had pulled two hundred dollars out of her wallet and handed it to me. I had no idea why I shouldn't get a job, but whatever.

After a couple days of lying on my bed, wallowing in despair, I'd realized that I needed to do something, anything, to stay busy and keep my mind off My Tragic Life. Hence my springing into action and becoming a domestic goddess.

Today I'd braved the heat and the wet, thick air to go out to get the mail—pathetically, getting the mail was the highlight of my day. Axelle got tons of catalogs, and I got a kick out of looking through them. Some of them sold freaky stuff for, like, pagans and "witches." I didn't know how anyone could take this stuff seriously, but she obviously did. I remembered how she'd run her fingers around my door frame after my nightmare. Had she been trying to do some kind of magic? How? What for?

Anyway. I loved her clothes catalogs, for the little bit of leather queen in all of us.

Sometimes I got letters from my friends or Mrs. Thompkins back home. Mostly we e-mailed, but they also sent me funny articles and pictures—which almost always made me cry.

I hadn't gotten anything from my dad's lawyer about his estate, and Mrs. Thompkins said they were still sorting through everything. It sounded like a total headache. I wanted it to be all settled—I could put the house furniture into storage, and when I escaped from this loony bin, I could set up my own apartment or house back home. I was counting the days.

Thais Allard, one envelope said. It was from the Orleans Parish Public School System. I ripped it open to find I was to attend École Bernardin, which was the nearest public school. It started in six days. Six days from now, a brand new school.

So, okay. I'd wanted to go to school, but somehow accepting the fact that I would attend school *here* felt like a ton of harsh reality all at once. An oh-so-familiar wave of despair washed over me as I headed up the narrow carriageway to the back of the building.

I went in, got blasted by the air-conditioning, and dumped Axelle's mail in a pile on the kitchen counter. A weird burning smell made me sneeze, and I followed it through the kitchen and into my bedroom, where Axelle was—get this—burning a little green branch and chanting.

"What the heck are you doing?" I asked, waving my arms to clear out the smoke.

"Burning sage," Axelle said briefly, and kept going, waving the smoldering green twigs in every corner of my room.

Burning sage? "You know, they make actual air fresheners," I said, dumping my stuff on my bed. "Or we could just open the window."

63

"This isn't for that," Axelle said. Her lips moved silently, and I finally got it: the burning sage was some "magic" thing she was doing. Like she was doing a "spell" in my room for some reason. So. This was my life: I lived with an unknown stranger who was right now performing a *voodoo* spell in my own *bedroom*. Because she actually believed all that crap. I mean, Jesus. Not to take the Lord's name in vain.

Axelle ignored me, murmuring some sort of chant under her breath as she moved about the room. In her other hand she held a crystal, like you can buy at a science shop, and she ran this around the window frame while she chanted.

I freaked. I couldn't help it. At that moment my life seemed so completely *insane*. Without saying a word, I turned around and ran out of that apartment, down the carriageway, and through the gate. Then I was on the narrow street, with slow-moving cars, tourists, street performers. It was all too much, and I pressed my hand against my mouth, trying not to cry. I hated this place! I wanted to be somewhere normal! I wanted to be home! While Welsford wasn't exactly a mime-free zone, still, I wouldn't encounter them on the street right outside my *house*.

My eyes blurred and I stumbled on the curb. I had nowhere to go, no refuge. Then the word *refuge* made me think of a church, and that made me remember a place I had seen a couple of days before: a small, hidden garden, behind a tall brick wall. It was attached to St. Peter's, a

Catholic church between Axelle's apartment and the small corner grocery store where I shopped.

I headed there now, walking fast down the brick-paved sidewalk. When I reached it, I pressed my face to the small iron grille inset into one wall, about five feet up. I walked the length of the brick wall and pushed some ivy aside to find a small wooden door, made for tiny Creole people of two centuries ago.

With no hesitation, I wrenched on the latch and shook the door hard until it popped open. Then I slipped under the ivy and entered a serene, private world.

The garden was small, maybe sixty feet square, and bordered by the church in back of it, an alley on one side, a parish office to the other side, and the street in front. But although all that separated me from the world was a seven-foot brick fence, this place was unnaturally quiet, set apart, not of the secular world somehow.

I glanced around. A few windows overlooked the garden, but I felt safe and private. Beneath a crape myrtle tree, its bark hanging off in silken shards, stood an ancient marble bench, and I sank down onto it, burying my face in my arms. I didn't make a sound, but hot tears squeezed out of my eyes and dripped into the crooks of my elbows. I expected someone to come tap me on the shoulder at any minute, telling me the garden was private and I had to leave, but no one did, and I lay hunched over that cool marble bench for a long time, my mind screaming variations of, *Someone, for God's sake, please help me.*

Finally, after my arms felt numb and one thigh had gone to sleep, I slowly straightened up. I felt waterlogged and puffy and sniffled, wiping my nose on my shirt-sleeve.

"Try this."

I jumped, startled, almost losing my balance over the back of the bench. To make my total humiliation complete, there was a guy about my age there, holding out a crisp white handkerchief.

"How long have you been there?" I demanded, all too aware of what I must look like: flush-faced, swollen eyes, Rudolph's nose.

"Long enough to know you could use a handkerchief," he said wryly, shaking it gently in front of me.

Okay. It was either that or blow my nose on my sleeve. Ungraciously I took the handkerchief and wiped my nose and dabbed at my eyes. Then what? Did one return a used hankie? Gross. The guy solved my dilemma by taking it from my hand and standing up. He walked to a small fountain that I hadn't even been aware of: a blue-caped, Nordic Virgin Mary, with thin streams of water running from her outstretched hands.

The guy wet the hankie and came back, wringing it out. I sighed and took it again, and since this situation was already too far gone for me to possibly salvage it, I wiped the cool, damp cloth over my face, feeling tons better.

"Thank you," I said, still unable to look at him.

"You're welcome." Uninvited, he sat down next to me. I was in no mood to make friends, so I just pretended he wasn't there. Now that I was calmer, I looked at the fountain, the different flowers growing in the somewhat untidy beds. Narrow walkways of well-worn brick made a knot of paths around the fountain. Small birds chirped in the thick growth of shrubs that hid the brick walls from inside.

The air was still humid here, marginally cooler than on the street. A vine grew thickly on several walls, its shiny dark green leaves surrounding heavily scented creamy flowers.

"Confederate jasmine," the guy said, as though he knew where I'd been looking. He knelt quickly and plucked a crisp white flower off a smaller shrub. Finally taking in his features, I saw that he had dark brown hair, almost black, and was tall, maybe almost six feet.

"Gardenia." He handed it to me, and I took it, inhaling its fragrance. It was almost unbearably sweet, too much scent for one flower to bear. But it was heavenly, and I tucked it behind my ear, which made the guy laugh lightly.

I managed to smile.

"I guess I'm trespassing," I said.

"I guess we both are," he agreed. "But I love to come here in the evenings, to escape the crowds and the heat."

"Do you work at the church?" I asked.

"No. But my apartment is right up there." He

pointed to the third story of the building next door. "I didn't mean to spy on you. But I thought you might be sick."

"No," I said glumly, thinking, *Sick of New Orleans.*

"I understand," he said gently. "Sometimes it's all too much." He had a precise, crisp way of speaking, as if he'd gone to school in England. I looked at him, into his eyes, and wondered if he *could* possibly understand.

No. Of course not. I got up and rewet the handkerchief in the fountain. I knelt by its base, wrung out the thin cloth, and wiped my face again and the back of my neck.

"I'll have to start carrying one of these," I said, pressing the wet cloth against my forehead.

"You're not used to the heat," he said.

"No. I'm from Connecticut," I said. "I've only been here a couple of weeks. I'm used to my air actually feeling like air."

He laughed, putting his head back. I realized that he was actually really good-looking, his throat smooth and tan, and I wondered if his chest was that color. I felt my face heat at that thought and looked down, embarrassed. When I looked up again, he was watching me intently.

"They say the heat makes people crazy," he said, his voice very quiet in the private garden. "That's why there are so many crimes of passion here—the unending heat works on you, frays your nerves. Next thing you know, your best friend has a knife to your throat."

Well, I was a *little* creeped out, but mostly his voice worked slowly through my veins like a drug, soothing me, calming me, taking away my raw pain.

"What did you do?" I asked seriously, and a glint of surprise lit his eyes for a moment.

He laughed again, and there was no mistaking it—I saw admiration in his eyes. Attraction. "I was speaking metaphorically. Fortunately, so far I haven't stolen my best friend's girl."

For just an instant, I pictured myself, going out with some unnamed best friend and then meeting this guy, feeling this electric attraction, and knowing that soon he would steal me away. I shivered.

"What's your name?" he asked, his words falling as softly as leaves.

"Thais," I said. Tye-ees.

He stood and offered me his hand. I looked up at him, his even features, the dark eyebrows slanting over incredible eyes. I took his hand. Unbelievably, he pressed my open palm against his lips, leaving a whisper of a kiss. "My pleasure, Thais," he said, awakening every nerve ending I had. "My name is Luc."

Luc, I repeated silently.

"Come here again soon," he said, looking at me as if to memorize my features. "I'll watch for you."

"I don't know when it will be," I hedged.

"It will be soon," he said confidently, and I knew that he was right.

I Have Sinned

"Forgive me, Father, for I have sinned." Marcel whispered the familiar words, anticipating the comfort of absolution. In this dark cubicle he was completely himself, and everything was all right. "It's been one week since my last confession."

"Have you any sins to confess, my son?"

Brother Eric. He was always understanding.

"Yes, Father," Marcel murmured. "I have ... felt anger. Great anger."

"Feeling anger in itself is not a sin, Marcel," Brother Eric said. "It is only when you enjoy the feeling of anger or act upon it."

"I fear ... were I to confront this anger, it could lead to ... violence." There, it was out.

"Violence?"

Marcel took a deep breath. "I have been contacted by former ... associates. I've tried to leave these people behind, Father. I've tried to escape them. I've come *here*. These people do not acknowledge the Lord our God. They play with ... fate. They have unholy power." Marcel felt his throat close. He shut his eyes, remembering that power, how it had flowed from his hands, how beautiful the world seemed when he held it.

"Explain about the violence, son," said Brother Eric.

"If I see them or one in particular—I'm afraid I will do him harm." A cold sweat broke out on Marcel's forehead. Yes, God was listening—but He might not be the only one. What a risk he was taking. . . . He looked around himself, contained in this dark cubicle.

"Do him harm out of anger?"

"Yes," said Marcel. "For trying to make me renounce what is good."

"Does he so threaten you, lad, that in order to protect yourself, you'd destroy him?"

"Yes," Marcel whispered.

"You don't see another path, Marcel?"

"I can never see him again," Marcel offered. "I can refuse to go to him, to help him."

"He's asked for your help?"

"Not yet. But I think he might. He's asked to see me."

"Perhaps he's changed his ways?" suggested Brother Eric.

"No," Marcel said with certainty.

"Then what does he want from you?"

"My . . . power." The words were so faint as to barely penetrate the wooden piercework screen.

"No one can take your power from you, Marcel."

Instantly Marcel saw that this was pointless, that Brother Eric could never understand, that there was no salvation for him here. He almost wept. He needed a strong hand to hold his, to say, *We will not let you go*. But the Church was all about free will. How to explain that sometimes, his will was not truly his own?

Liar. His conscience was a small, cold voice, mocking him inside his head. *Your will is your own. You like the power, Marcel. You like wielding it. You love feeling life, energy, pure force flowing from you, from your hands. You like what you can do with it. You like what you can do to others.*

"No! No, I don't! You're lying," Marcel cried, covering his face with his hands.

"Marcel?"

It doesn't have to be bad, Marcel, said his conscience. *Remember, "There is nothing either good or bad, but thinking makes it so." You can use your power for good. You can convince the others. They want to be good anyway. It's only Daedalus—Daedalus and Jules and Axelle. Maybe Manon. Maybe Richard. But the others, they're for good. They follow the Bonne Magie. You can too. Your power could elevate them to goodness.*

"No, no," Marcel sobbed as the velvet curtain opened and Brother Eric touched his shoulder. "I can't go back."

"Marcel, we must all face our demons," Brother Eric said softly. "Now come, rest. You've been working too hard. I'll have Brother Simon bring you some soup."

Marcel let himself be led out of the chapel, its stones standing watch over God's disciples since 1348. But Marcel knew they could no longer protect him. It was only a matter of time. Every step he took was a step closer to his own personal hell, and whatever awaited him in New Orleans.

Clio

"**Y**ou're late." I gave Andre the full force of my "peeved" look, which made lesser guys quake. Andre just grinned and swooped in to kiss my neck, which pretty much shorted out all rational thought.

"So we're even, then," he said, with such an unrepentant, wicked expression on his face that I laughed and couldn't hold it against him. Instead I pushed against his chest, barely moving him, and then walked ahead, trying to get my fluttering nerves under control. My palms tingled where I'd touched him.

"You're lucky I waited," I tossed over my shoulder.

Andre caught up to me, matching his steps with mine. It was dusk, the sun just beginning to set over the bend of the Mississippi River. It was a magickal time. I mean, literally magickal, when the force of the sun was yielding to the force of the moon. Some rites used this time on purpose to harness the effects of both.

"This is a pretty park," he said.

I looked around. The small golf course had been molded with weensy, artificial hills. Huge live oaks towered over us, spreading shade beneath their branches. It was so familiar to me that I barely noticed anymore. "I like how green New Orleans is," I said. "My grandmother and I went to Arizona a couple of years ago, and it was awful. I mean, actually, it was pretty, in a really dry, dusty way. But I felt parched somehow. I like being surrounded by green."

I pressed my lips together. *Déesse*, I sounded like a freaking idiot. Or a travel guide. What was wrong with me? Why did he throw me off balance? I took a deep breath, momentarily closed my eyes. *Center. Center myself.*

"Come this way," I said, holding out my hand.

Andre took it, his skin warm against mine. "Where are you leading me?"

Everything he said seemed to have two meanings. He could make anything sound sexy or forbidden.

I smiled back at him, pulling him along. Years ago, Racey and I had found a place we called our clubhouse. Really, it was just a dip in the ground, between the massive roots of three live oaks. If you lay flat, no one could see you until they were right on top of you. We used to lie there for hours, talking, practicing little baby spells, giggling to ourselves when we heard passing golfers swear and throw down their clubs.

Now, standing at the entrance, I suddenly remembered my horrible vision—the one where blood had bubbled up from between a tree's roots. But that had been a cypress tree. I swallowed hard and forced myself to step over the large roots. It had just been a dumb vision—you could see all kinds of freaky stuff when you let your magick rip. I wasn't going to think about it.

I sat down, tucking my skirt under me. It was lavender and tiered, almost reaching my ankles, long and flowing. Guys loved stuff like that. On top I wore a little white cotton camisole that buttoned up the back and had embroidered lavender butterflies. I'd worn my hair in two braids to get it off my neck.

I kicked off my sandals and patted the ground next to me.

"You should feel honored. You're the first non-blood sister to see this place," I said teasingly, tapping his knee with a long piece of centipede grass.

He looked at me quickly. "Blood sister?"

I nodded solemnly. "My best friend, Racey, and I are blood sisters—we did a rite when we were ten. I think I still have the scar." I looked at my thumb, but the tiny cut where I had shared my blood with Racey's had long become invisible.

"She was with you at Botanika," Andre said, leaning back on his elbows. He was wearing a blue oxford shirt that looked incredibly soft and worn. The sleeves were rolled halfway up to his elbows. Like his shirt, his khaki cargo shorts were well broken in, the fabric velvety.

"Yes." I looked up to find him smiling knowingly at me. Without even really thinking about it, the words sprang into my mind: *I am the woman you desire, my will is strong, my passion's fire. I will give myself to you, once you prove that you are true.*

It wasn't a proper spell, not really. There was no real intent in my mind, I had no tools, and I wasn't even trying to achieve any specific thing. It was more . . . opening his mind to the idea. Allowing him to see me as his true love. Sort of moving things along, in a way.

He blinked once, quickly, and looked at me, almost as if he'd heard my thought, which was impossible. But that's how finely we were already attuned to each other, that he could somehow sense something, some strong emotion flowing from me.

"How are you liking the local scenery?" he asked, echoing my words to him the first time we met.

I swallowed, feeling shivery and excited. "I'm liking it," I said, and my voice sounded a little rough, a little unsure. Perfect.

"Come here," he said, his face intent, his slight French accent making his *h* almost silent.

Moments later, it was just like at Amadeo's. We fit together perfectly, and for the first time in my life, I felt actually overwhelmed. Before, no matter who I was with, part of my brain was always doing an imaginary manicure, or going over a lesson with Nan, or thinking about clothes I wanted to buy. This time all my senses were focused on Andre, the way he felt, tasted, the scent of his skin, the heat in his hands as he held me. *This is the one,* I thought. *I'm only seventeen, and I've found my one perfect love.* It was amazing and also a tiny bit scary. All my emotions made perfect sense to me, but there was a tiny part of me that was still marveling at how strongly I felt about him so quickly. But I couldn't stop it—I was caught on this swift ride of emotion, and there was no way to slow it down. I didn't even want to.

I couldn't help smiling against his lips with happiness, and he pulled back to look at me.

"What's funny?" he asked, looking at me.

"Not funny," I said, pressing my hips against him. "Happy."

"Happy?"

I laughed at his confused expression. "Yes, *happy*." I raised my eyebrows. "Or are you not happy to be here with me?"

"No." He smiled. "I'm happy." He traced my eyebrow with one finger, letting it trail down my cheek. "Happy to be here with you." He leaned back so he was lying next to me and looked up at the sky. Never in my life had any boy ever stopped kissing me *himself*. It wasn't all physical with Andre—he wanted to be with me for more than just that. He was so much *deeper* than anyone else I'd ever known, and my heart swelled. I looked at his beautiful profile, like a classical statue's, and felt like the luckiest person in the world.

"Tell me about yourself," he said, still gazing at the thicket of oak leaves overhead. The growing darkness made it even more private. "Who do you live with?"

I laughed. "What kind of a question is that? You don't think I live with my parents?"

He looked at me curiously. "Oh. And do you?" Maybe he'd been hoping I had a roommate, my own place, and I suddenly felt stupid, childish.

"Actually, no," I said. "I live with my grandmother. I always have."

"It's very sad to lose your parents so young," he said, turning on his side to face me. He took my hand and held it in his own against his chest. I could feel his heart beating. I wondered why he'd assumed that I had actually *lost* my parents—they could have been divorced, or in prison, or maybe just one of them was dead.

I shook my head. I'd *told* him I'd always lived with my grandmother—of course it sounded like I'd never had any parents.

"What about you?" I asked. "Where's your family from?"

"My parents died a long time ago too," he said. "But some of my extended family still lives in France—a little town called St. Malo."

"I would love to go to France," I said dreamily. *Hint, hint.* "My family was originally from there, a couple hundred years ago. I'd love to go visit."

"You've never been there?"

"No." I looked into his dark blue eyes. "I bet it's so beautiful there. Bet it has good food."

Andre smiled easily and tapped my lip with one gentle finger. "Yes. Very good food. Who knows? Maybe one day we'll see France together."

Yes! "I'd like that," I said, and put my hand on his neck, beneath the collar of his shirt. I drew his head toward me and kissed him again. "I can see us doing lots of things together," I whispered.

He kissed me back, pressing my shoulders into the soft ground. His dark head blotted out the day's final bit of light, and I closed my eyes. Andre kissed my eyelids, my forehead, my cheeks, my birthmark, my chin, and I lay quietly, smiling, soaking it all up. I was filled with happiness and felt the rush of love and light and power swell inside me. I so wished I could make real magick, a proper spell, right there—I knew I'd be more powerful than ever before. I would try to hold on to this feeling when I went home. Nan would be impressed. The power of love.

Someday I would be able to show Andre who and what I was. If he loved me as deeply as I loved him, then magick would be just another experience for us to share, another aspect of my life I would open to him.

His hand moved slowly from my waist over my camisole, and my muscles went taut as it brushed lightly over my breast. I shuddered, eyes closed, holding him tightly, feeling his knee press between mine.

"Come home with me." The words were barely whispered against my temple.

Everything in me said yes. I pictured us alone and private. I saw his skin against mine, us joining completely, how magickal it would be. All it would take was for me to stand up, take his hand, and go to his apartment. Then we could be together.

I didn't want to open my eyes. If I kept my eyes shut, I could still imagine us together, see how it would be.

"Clio?"

I sighed and opened my eyes. It was dark out. Cicadas were thrumming rhythmically around us.

"Clio. Come." Andre stroked wisps of my hair back

against my temple. I felt my heartbeat echo everywhere he touched.

"I can't."

His dark eyebrows raised, and the phrase *handsome as the devil* popped into my mind. "What?" He looked taken aback, and I felt angry at reality, resentful, and . . . bound to obey Nan.

I licked my lips. "I'm sorry, Andre. Tonight I can't. Another time? Any other time, practically. But—"

"I've pushed you." He looked regretful.

"No! It isn't that at all," I said. "I've pushed you as much as you've pushed me." I swallowed hard, my blood still running strong and hot with longing. "It's so stupid. But tomorrow is the first day of school. Believe it or not. And even though everything in me wants to just be with you— still, my grandmother would absolutely kill me if I came home really late on the night before school started."

I felt my face flush even more, if possible. I, Clio Martin, felt so incredibly uncool, for perhaps the first time in my life. Ninety-eight percent of me said to blow Nan off, to go with Andre, to seize life, etc. But the other two percent held powerful sway: I loved Nan, and I hated disappointing her or making her angry.

Andre was expressionless, propped up on one elbow, looking down at me. For a few moments I felt so acutely horrible that I was absolutely ready to jump up and grab Andre's hand and say I was just kidding.

I sat up fast. "Actually, I—" I began, just as Andre said, "I understand."

"What?" I stared at him, his face with its strong bones.

"I understand," he repeated. He smiled ruefully. "Of course you need to get home. I wasn't thinking—I'm sorry. I was listening to my heart and not my head."

I blinked, astonished to feel the beginnings of tears in my eyes. Could Andre be more perfect? He was everything wild and dangerous and sexy that I could ever hope for, and he was *also* caring, unselfish, and considerate.

I took his strong tan hand and kissed it. He smiled and looked boyishly pleased.

"Come," he said. "I'll take you home."

I hesitated. Something in me didn't want Nan to meet him just yet. She always asked questions about the guys I dated, and I wanted to know Andre a little better before I went through the inquisition. Besides, she'd have plenty of time to get used to him as her future grandson-in-law.

I shook my head. "I can walk from here. It's perfectly safe." Since I could zap a freezing spell on any jerk who messed with me.

He frowned. "No, Clio, please—let me see you home."

I shook my head and stood up, brushing the leaves off my clothes. "I get out of school at three," I told him. "Can I see you tomorrow?"

He laughed and pulled me to him. "You can see me anytime you want."

Thais

I lay in bed, wondering what I should do first: cry or throw up. It seemed pointless to "wake up," since I'd been staring at my ceiling, sleepless, pretty much all night. Today was my first day of school in a new place. The first day of school in my whole life that my dad wouldn't be there to take me, holding my hand when I was little, waving goodbye when I got older. I felt intensely alone, waking up in this strange apartment, everything so foreign around me.

My eyelids felt like sandpaper. I rolled over in bed, hugging my pillow. Ever since my nightmare, I'd been hating falling asleep. Axelle insisted I keep the door to my room open, and on the one hand, I actually appreciated her being able to hear me if I cried out. On the other hand, I sorely missed my privacy and the implied safety of a locked door. Especially when Jules and Daedalus stayed over, which they did every once in a while.

I sleepwalked to the bathroom and got under the shower. In New Orleans, the cold water was never actually cold, like in Connecticut. Back home, the C on the faucet meant business. Here the C meant "tepid"—I never even bothered with hot water.

And another thing: back home, the first day of school always meant new school clothes, autumny clothes. School starts: autumn's on the way. The forecast for today was a high of ninety-six, one hundred percent humidity. I wore a short skirt and a sleeveless top, both gray with pink athletic stripes. I guessed I would soon find out what was considered cool to wear here.

I spritzed my hair and bunched it up to make the layers stand out. I started crying. I put drops in my eyes and tried to put on mascara. I started crying again. I quit with the makeup and headed out to the kitchen. So now only throwing up was left.

In the main room, I found Axelle, Jules, and Daedalus sitting around the table, wearing the same clothes from last night. The ashtray was full of cigarettes. Empty soda cans and bottles of water circled the table. They had clearly been up all night, and I was amazed they hadn't been louder.

"Hey," I said unenthusiastically, and they looked up.

"You're up early," Axelle said, glancing at the antique clock on the mantel.

"School," I said, trying to eat a plain piece of bread.

Axelle let out a breath, giving Jules and Daedalus a meaningful look. I was so zany and unpredictable, wanting to go to school.

"You were *serious* about that," she muttered. Then, "What time will you be home?"

"School gets out at three," I said, chewing, struggling

to swallow. "I guess around three thirty? I don't know how long the streetcar will take."

"Give her a cell phone," Daedalus told Axelle, and I stopped chewing in surprise.

She looked at him, her black eyes thoughtful. Then she stood, fished around in her huge black leather purse, and pulled out a cell phone. For a moment she stood looking at it, tracing her fingers over it as if, like, memorizing it, saying goodbye. To a cell phone. Jeez.

Finally she brought it over to me. I couldn't believe it.

"Let us know if you're going to be late," she said.

O-kaaay. And you'll have cookies hot from the oven ready for me, right?

I had bought myself a backpack and stocked it with a few first-day supplies. I zipped the phone into a little pocket.

"Thais, come here," Jules said, and I walked over. Now what?

The three of them were hunched over all kinds of old maps and new maps and books and what looked like geographical surveys.

"Have you ever seen anything like this before?" Axelle asked. Though she'd been up all night, she didn't look beat. Her skin was clear, her eyes bright—even her makeup looked okay.

"Maps? Yeah—I've seen *maps* before." I had no idea what she meant.

"No, more—maps like this," she said, pulling one out. It looked like an olde-timey reproduction on fake parchment, the edges tattered. I expected to see a big black *X* somewhere, where the treasure was buried.

I shook my head. "Like a pirate map? Not any real ones."

Jules snorted with laughter, and Axelle looked irritated.

"Not a pirate map," she said. "Old maps. *Real* old maps. Did your father have anything like this among his things? Did you ever see anything else like this when you were little?"

Well, that ranked right up there as being one of the weirder questions I'd ever been asked. "No." I shook my head again and started moving toward the door. "Dad didn't have anything like that. See you later."

I slipped out the door into the lush, damp courtyard. It was early—I'd allowed plenty of time to get to school by public transportation—but already incredibly, jungle-style hot. Before I'd even reached the side gate, I felt damp and limp. Great. I swallowed the last of my bread, feeling it stick in my throat. Somehow, this morning, I missed my dad even more than yesterday.

Clio

"You ready?" I glanced over at Racey, who held up one finger and sucked down the last of her coffee.

"I guess so." She leaned down and grabbed her retro plaid backpack, then leaned back against the car seat and closed her eyes. "I'm not ready," she moaned.

I leaned back and closed my eyes too. I'd already shut off the Camry's engine, so it was going to get hot in here in about two seconds, but we needed to take a moment. "Yeah," I said. "Where did the summer go?"

"We got to the beach, what, once?" Racey complained.

I thought back to the long, hot summer days and the long, hot summer nights. "Still, we had some fun," I pointed out. "And I met Andre."

"Yeah." Racey opened her eyes and looked out the window. Some of our other friends were already gathered around the cement bench in front of the "Friendship Tree." Racey and I were the only witches in our group, but it wasn't a secret. There have always been witches in New Orleans, so it wasn't a big deal. Witches, Catholics, voodoo, Santeria, Jews—there was a lot of latitude about acceptable religions. Our friends thought it was kind of a hobby rather than a whole system of power. I didn't correct them.

Racey looked down at her nails, which were painted black with little white lightning bolts on them.

"Your nails match your hair," I realized.

She grinned at me. "I know I've got kind of a skunk thing going, but I like it." She took a deep breath and let it out, then unlocked her door. "Okay, I'm ready. Let's go rock this joint."

Laughing, I got out and unsuccessfully tugged my tank top down so it would meet my board shorts. Surely the school couldn't enforce their quaint "dress code" ideas today, not in this heat.

"Yo!" called Eugenie LaFaye, holding up a hand in greeting.

"So you got home all right that Saturday?" Della asked with a smirk. The last time I'd seen her, I'd been trying to remember where the hell I'd left my car in a mall parking lot. That day felt like ages and ages ago—it was hard to believe I'd known Andre for such a short time. He'd changed my life so much, it was like his appearance had separated my history into two parts: before him and after him.

"Oh, sure," I said airily. "How many blue, 1998 Toyota Camrys could there possibly be in a mall parking lot? Like, two thousand?"

"Yeah, and she found hers after only one thousand, three hundred and seventy-eight," Racey said, and they all laughed.

"So we got lucky," I said brightly.

"We've been checking out the talent," said Nicole, nodding at a bunch of guys over by the basketball hoops. Racey's little brother, Trey, was among them.

I looked over but without a lot of interest. Ordinarily, of course, my antennae would be quivering—gauging the guys, obsessing over what I was wearing, seeing who was checking me out, enjoying being able to stun guys with a look, a word. Now even the most studly senior guys looked like second graders. Realizing I was already feeling clammy at eight forty-five in the morning, I twisted my hair into a knot, fished a chopstick out of my backpack, and stuck it through. "Voilà," I said. "Chic yet simple."

"Goofy yet messy," Eugenie said in the same tone.

"Ladies," said a voice, and I turned to see Kris Edwards stroll up.

"Hey, girl," I said, giving her a hug. "And how were the Swiss Alps?" Kris's family was stinking rich, and she'd spent the summer in Europe.

"Swissy," she said, hugging Racey next. "Alpy."

"And the Swiss lads?" Nicole asked. "Your IMs left much to the imagination."

"For which we're thankful," I said, and Kris laughed.

"The Swiss talent was very . . . talented," she said, smirking, and Della slapped her a high five. "And you?" she asked me. "Racey IM'ed that you'd met someone tall, dark, and dangerous."

"Dangerous?" I looked at Racey, who shrugged, looking

a little embarrassed. "Well, he's tall, dark, and *fabulous*, but he's not dangerous. His name is Andre," I said, trying unsuccessfully not to look too smug.

"Ooh, *Andre*," said Nicole, just as the first morning bell rang.

"He's French," I said. "With a real French accent. He could read the phone book and I'd be drooling." We started moving toward the side doors, following the stream of other students. As usual, the freshmen looked like they should be in sixth grade. I was sure we'd never looked that young.

"I love French accents," Della said enviously.

"He *is* incredibly good-looking," Racey said loyally, and I smiled at her.

"Okay, let's see who we've got for homerooms," Kris said, and we headed for the senior lists on the walls.

I looked, but my mind wasn't on it. I kept thinking about lying with Andre beneath the tree and how sure I was that we were meant to be together. It was a completely different feeling than I'd ever had, and it changed everything—school, friends, my whole world. I felt older somehow. Two weeks ago I'd been another seventeen-year-old about to start senior year. Now senior year was just a stepping-stone to the rest of my life and the person I wanted to spend it with. It was weird: I felt somehow calmer and more sure than I'd ever felt but also more excited and full of anticipation than I'd ever felt. Two weeks ago I'd been just like all my friends. Now I had this huge relationship, and they didn't. And it made me different from them forever.

Thais

The streetcar stopped right across the street from École Bernardin. I'd been practically hanging out the open window, totally nervous that I would somehow miss it. I felt more alone than I ever had in my whole life, even when a bunch of other kids got off the streetcar with me, obviously going to the same school.

I know it's always hard being the new kid—I mean, I'd *read* about it. But I'd never *been* the new kid before. And from the looks I was getting, this school didn't seem to get too many new kids. Some people glanced at me and gave me casual waves or smiles, but others stared at me like I was an alien—edging me closer to nervous-breakdown-dom.

The school building looked like it had been built back in the sixties, painted garish shades of blue and orange. Inside, one of the first doors I saw said GIRLS, and I ducked in there fast. Three sinks sat below three mirrors, and I looked at myself to see if I had toothpaste on my face or had grown horns or something.

I was still trying to figure it out when a girl emerged from a cubicle and stood next to me to wash her hands.

She glanced casually at me in the mirror and said, "Oh, hey—" Then she stopped and actually did a double take.

"*What?*" I asked, my nerves about to snap. "What's wrong with me?"

"Uh . . ." The girl looked totally taken aback. "Uh, who *are* you? Are you new here?"

"Yes," I said, crossing my arms over my chest. "Do you guys never get new people? Everyone's looking at me like I have two heads. What *is* it?" I swallowed hard, praying that I wouldn't start crying.

The girl shook her head. "Nothing's wrong with you," she said, trying to be nice. "But it's just that you—you really look like someone who already goes to school here."

I stared at her, thinking of the few casual "heys" I'd gotten. "*What?* I look *so* similar to someone that people are *staring* at me when I go by? You've got to be kidding."

"No," the girl said, giving me an apologetic smile. "You really do look like her. It's kind of weird, actually."

I didn't know what to say. Once again I had entered some crazy New Orleans X-Files where the rules of reality didn't apply.

"I'm sorry," the girl said, and held out her hand. "I'm Sylvie. Do you want me to show you where the office is?"

I shook her hand, feeling a pathetic amount of relief that I'd met someone kind. "I'm Thais," I said. "That would be great."

Just walking beside Sylvie helped so much, to the point where I could quit freaking out and actually pay attention to the reactions I was getting. It wasn't from everyone—mostly older kids. I saw what Sylvie meant: some kids said hello, as if they already knew me. Others looked like they were going to say hi, then frowned and looked confused.

"Okay, here it is," said Sylvie, showing me to an open door by a wide counter. Clearly the school office. "Homerooms are by last name. What's yours?"

"Allard," I said, and she smiled and nodded.

"I'm Allen—Sylvie Allen! So we'll be in the same one. I'll see you soon, okay?"

"Thanks," I said gratefully.

Sylvie nodded and headed down the hall, and I waited at the counter. A middle-aged woman with curly gray hair came over to me.

"Yes, Clio?" she said briefly, taking out a form from under the counter. "What can I do for you?"

There was no one standing there but me. "Um, I'm not Clio," I said.

The woman stopped and looked at me full-on. Embarrassed, I stood there, feeling like a zoo exhibit. A bell rang, and the halls filled with even more kids. The bell stopped, and still she hadn't said anything to me.

"You're not Clio," she said finally.

"No. Someone told me I look like someone who already goes to school here." *But can you get over it?* "Here are my transcripts from my last school." I pushed them across the counter. "I just moved here this summer. From Connecticut."

Slowly she took my transcripts and the registration letter I'd gotten in the mail. Her name tag said Ms. DiLiberti. "Thais Allard," she said, pronouncing it correctly.

"Yes."

"Yes, well, welcome, Thais," she said, seeming to recover enough to give me a professional smile. "I see you were a very good student back in Connecticut. I'm sure you'll do well here."

"Thank you."

"Your homeroom teacher will be Ms. Delaney, room 206. You'll just take the first set of stairs over there to your left."

"Thanks."

"And here's some other information." Now she was all business. "Here's a copy of our school handbook—you might find that helpful. Here's our school contract—please read it, sign it, and get it back to me by the end of the day. And if you could fill in this emergency contact form."

"Yes, okay." This stuff I could deal with. What a relief. Then something almost imperceptible made my shoulders tense. I looked up just in time to see Ms. DiLiberti straighten, looking over my shoulder.

"Wait," she said to me. "Clio!"

I looked around—at last, they'd see us both together and we could stop all this double-take crap. A group of girls was walking toward us, laughing among themselves.

The light was behind them, so they were just dark silhouettes.

"Clio! Clio Martin!" Ms. DiLiberti called.

I turned to face the counter, suddenly aware of a shaky feeling in the pit of my stomach. It was barely nine o'clock, and I was exhausted and emotionally wrung out. *Just meet Clio and get it over with.* But still, I felt nervous and anxious all over again.

"See y'all," said a voice. *It sounded like my voice*— except the word *y'all* would never pass my lips. A fist of something like dread grabbed my stomach. I didn't know why I felt this way, but I was barely able to keep it together. "Yes, Ms. DiLiberti? It wasn't me," said the voice. "I just got here."

Ms. DiLiberti smiled wryly. "Amazingly, I haven't called you over to discuss your latest transgression," she said. "After all, it's only nine o'clock on the first day. I'll give you a little more time. But there's someone I want you to meet. Thais?"

Slowly I turned, finally face-to-face with the mysterious—

Me.

I blinked, and for one second I almost put up a hand to see if someone had slipped a mirror in front of me. My eyes widened, and identical green eyes widened simultaneously. My mouth opened a tiny bit, and a mouth shaped like mine but with slightly darker lip gloss also opened. I stepped back automatically and quickly scanned this other me, this Clio.

Our hair was different—hers was longer, I guessed, since it was in a messy knot on the back of her head. Mine was feathered in layers above my shoulders. She was wearing a white tank top and pink-and-red surfer shorts that laced up the front. She had a silver belly ring. We had the same long legs, the same arms. She had a slightly darker tan. We were the same height and looked like we were the same weight, or almost. And here was the really, really unbelievable part:

We had the exact same strawberry birthmark, shaped like a crushed flower. Only hers was on her left cheekbone, and mine was on the right. We were *identical*, two copies of the same person, peeled apart at some point to make mirror images of each other.

Even though my brain was screaming in confusion, one coherent thought surfaced: there was only one possible explanation.

Clio was my twin sister.

Clio

"Oh. My. Freaking. God." I was vaguely aware the voice was mine, but everything else had faded away. The only thing in my universe just then was this girl, who had obviously been cloned from my DNA. Obvious—but impossible.

Racey quickly looked at me, then at the other me, and she literally gasped. "Holy Mother," she breathed.

The other me looked like someone had just put a binding spell on her—frozen in place, eyes open wide, muscles stiff. Then I noticed one difference between us.

"Your face is green," I said, just as her eyelids fluttered and she started to collapse.

Racey and I caught her, and Ms. DiLiberti hustled out from behind the counter and led us into the assistant principal's office. Someone got a wet paper towel. I fanned the new girl's face with a copy of the student handbook.

Almost immediately, she opened her eyes and sat up, though she was still kind of whitish green around the edges.

I hadn't taken my eyes off her. *So that's what I would look like with layered hair,* I thought, realizing I felt stunned and not enjoying the experience. My heart was beating hard, and a million thoughts pushed insistently at my brain. I didn't want to let them in.

"Who *are* you?" I asked. "Where are you from? Why are you here?"

She drank some water that Ms. DiLiberti brought her and pushed her hair off her face. "I'm Thais Allard," she said, sounding almost exactly like me but more Yankeeish. "I'm from Connecticut. My dad died this summer, and my new guardian lives here, so I moved here."

Her dad died. *Who was he?* I wanted to shout. Had that been my dad too? Had we been separated at birth and Thais adopted by strangers? Or maybe I—was Nan my nan? She had to be. But she'd never, ever mentioned that I might have a sister. And this girl, even if she was from the planet Xoron, had to be my sister. We were just too freakishly identical, down to our matching *birthmarks*. The birthmark that I'd alternately loved and hated, the one Andre had traced, had kissed just yesterday—was on her face.

"Who was your dad?" I said. "Who's your new guardian?"

Thais wavered and looked like she was about to turn on the faucets. Outside the office, we heard other students coming and going.

"I'm going to be late for homeroom," she said faintly, and I thought, Sacrée mère, *she's a weenie.*

"Your teachers will understand," Ms. DiLiberti said firmly.

"My dad was Michel Allard," the girl said. I'd never heard of him. "My new guardian is some weird friend of his." She shrugged, frowning.

It was all too much to take in. I felt a little weak-kneed myself, but unlike The Fainter, I sagged gracefully into a chair.

The girl—Thais—seemed to be coming back to life. "Do you have parents?" I saw the sudden eagerness on her face, and it was only then that I realized that Nan *had* to be her grandmother too. I would have to *share* Nan.

I'm a successful only child. I mean, I'm successful at *being* an only child. I bit my lip and said, "I live with my grandmother. My parents are dead." *Our* parents were dead. "When's your birthday?" I asked brusquely.

"November twenty-second." Now her eyes were examining me, her strength coming back. *Déesse*, was she even a *witch*? Well, of course, she had to be—but did she grow up being a witch? How could she not?

I frowned. "I'm November twenty-*first*." I looked up at Racey to find her staring at me, like, what the hell is going on? Such a good question. One that I intended to ask Nan as soon as possible. I thought—Nan was probably not home now. She was a midwife, a nurse-practitioner at a local clinic. She had irregular hours, but she'd been getting ready to leave when I was walking out the door this morning.

"Where were you born?" Thais asked me.

"Here, New Orleans," I said. "Weren't you?"

Thais frowned. "No—I was born in Boston."

Racey raised her eyebrows. "That must have been a neat trick."

The first-period bell rang. I couldn't remember a time when I'd felt less like going to class, which in my case was saying something. All I wanted to do was go home and confront Nan, ask her why a stranger had shown up at *my* school in *my* town with *my* face. I'd just have to wait till she got back tonight.

"Well, this is certainly a mystery," said Ms. DiLiberti, standing up. "You two obviously have some figuring out to do. But right now I'm going to write you passes for your teachers, and you're going to get to your first-period classes."

I consulted my class schedule. "I have American history."

Thais looked at hers. She still seemed shaken and pale, which made her birthmark stand out like red ink on her cheek. "I have senior English."

"You girls get going," said Ms. DiLiberti briskly, handing us pink slips. "You too, Racey. And I can't wait to hear how this all plays out."

"Me neither," I muttered, gathering my stuff.

"Me neither," said Thais, sounding like an instant replay of me.

"Me neither," said Racey, and Thais looked at her, seeming to notice her for the first time. "I'm Racey Copeland," she told Thais.

"I don't know who I am," Thais said in a small voice,

99

and suddenly I kind of felt sorry for her. And for me. For both of us.

"We're going to find out," I said.

Nan didn't come home until almost six o'clock. When she works late, I'm in charge of dinner, which we call emergency dinners, because cooking is yet another domestic art I'm not strong at.

Tonight's emergency dinner was a frozen pizza and a salad. I ripped up a head of lettuce and got a tomato from the garden in back. Ta da.

From the moment I'd walked in the door, I'd been wound as tight as a window shade. My shoulders literally ached. This afternoon I'd planned to see Andre—I'd finally been going to go to his apartment, and who knew what would happen? But now all I could think about was the fact that my double was walking around New Orleans, looking like me, sounding like me, yet not being me. I mean, it wasn't her fault, obviously, but I felt like a Versace bag that had suddenly seen a vinyl imitation being sold on a street corner.

So I just paced around the house, my jaw aching from being clenched, missing Andre and wanting to run to him and have him make me forget all about this and instead counting the minutes until my grandmother got home.

Finally I felt her pushing open the front gate. I didn't go meet her but waited while she turned her key in the lock and came in. She looked tired, but when she saw my face, she straightened up, very alert.

"What is it?" she said. "What's happened?"

And that was when Clio Martin, stoic queen, non-crier in public, non-crier in general, burst into tears and fell on her shoulder.

Nan was so startled it took a moment for her to put her arms around me.

I pulled back and looked at her. "I'm a *twin!*" I cried. "I have an identical twin!"

To say I'd managed to take Nan by surprise was a gross understatement. I had absolutely floored her, and believe me, Nan did not floor easily. She'd always seemed like she'd seen everything, that nothing could rock her or make her upset. Even in second grade, when I'd slipped on a watermelon seed and split my head open on our neighbor's cement porch, Nan had simply filled a dish towel with ice, told me to hold it in place, and driven me to the hospital.

But this, *this* had really managed to stun her. Her face turned white, her eyes were dark and huge in her face, and she actually staggered back. "What?" she said weakly.

Okay, now—most people, if they went home and told their grandmother they were a twin, the grandmother would laugh and say, "Oh, you are *not.*"

So this was not good.

Nan wobbled backward and I stuck a chair under her just in time. She grabbed my hands and held them and said, "Clio, what are you talking about?"

I sat down in another chair, still sobbing. "There's

another me at school! This morning they called me to the office, and there was *me*, standing there, but with a haircut! Nan, I mean, we're *identical!* We're exactly alike except she's a Yankee, and she even has my exact same *birthmark!* I mean, what the hell is *going on?*" My last words ended in a totally un-Clio-like shriek.

Nan looked like she'd seen a ghost, only I bet if she saw a real ghost, it wouldn't faze her. She swallowed, still speechless.

Something was so, so wrong with this picture. I felt like the two of us were sitting there, waiting for a hurricane to hit our house, to yank it right off its foundation, to sweep us up with it. I quit crying and just gaped at her, thinking, *Oh my God, oh my God, oh my God. She knew.*

"Nan—" I said, and then stopped.

She seemed to come back to herself then, shaking her head and focusing on me. A tiny bit of color leached back into her face, but she still looked pretty whacked. "Clio," she said, in this old, old voice. "She had your same birthmark?"

I nodded and touched my cheekbone. "Hers is on the other side. It's exactly like mine. Nan—*tell me.*"

"What's her name?" Nan's voice was thin and strained, barely more than a whisper.

"Thais Allard," I said. "She said her dad had just died, and now she lives here with a friend of her dad's. She used to live in Connecticut. She says she was born in Boston but the day after me."

Nan put her fingers to her lips. I saw her soundlessly form the name *Thais*. "Michel is dead?" she asked sadly, as if from far away.

"*You* knew him? Was that—he wasn't *my* real dad, was he? Wasn't he just someone who adopted *Thais*?" I felt like my sanity was about to rip in half. "Nan, explain this to me. *Now*."

At last, her eyes sparked with recognition. She looked at me with her familiar, sharp gaze, and I could recognize her again.

"Yes," she said, her voice firmer. "Yes, of course, *cher*. I'll explain. I'll explain everything. But first—first there are some things I must do, very quickly."

While I sat with my jaw hanging open like a large-mouth bass, she sprang to her feet with her usual energy. She hurried into our workroom, and I heard the cupboard open. I sat there, unable to move, to process anything except a series of cataclysmic thoughts: I had a sister, a twin sister. I'd had a father, maybe, until this summer. I'd have to share Nan. Nan had been lying to me my whole life.

Over and over, those thoughts burned a pattern into my brain.

Numbly I watched Nan come out, dressed in a black silk robe, the one she wore for serious work or when it was her turn to lead our coven's monthly circle. She held her wand, a slim length of cypress no thicker than my pinkie. She didn't look at me but quickly centered herself and started chanting in old French, only a few words of which I recognized. Her first coven, Balefire, had always worked in a kind of language all their own, she'd told me—a mixture of old French, Latin, and one of the African dialects brought here during the dark days of slavery.

She went outside, and I felt her circling our house, our yard. She came onto the porch and stood before our front door. She came back inside and moved through each room, tracing each window with a crystal, singing softly in a language that had been passed down by our family for hundreds of years.

Every now and then I caught a word, but even before then it had sunk in what she was doing.

She was weaving layer after layer of spells all around our house, our yard, around us, around our lives.

Spells of protection and ward-evil.

Life at the Golden Blossom

Sunlight was a painful thing, Claire thought, trying to drag a sheet over her eyes. But thin pinpricks of morning seared her retinas, and she knew it was pointless to hold it off any longer.

Carefully she pried one eyelid open. The hazy view of her broken wooden window screen showed her it was maybe only two in the afternoon. Not too bad.

The bed was sunken weirdly—she was rolling toward the middle. A survey revealed a human form sleeping next to her, his straight black hair tossed across a pillow. No one she recognized. Well, that happened.

She sighed. A bath would revive her, and no one did baths better than the Golden Blossom hotel.

"Please, ma'am?"

Claire willed her head to turn and somehow managed to switch her gaze a bit to the left. A small Thai maid, no more than fifteen, knelt on the black wooden floor. She held up a silver tray covered with a stack of neatly folded telephone messages. Her head was bowed—she was reluctant to disturb ma'am. Especially this ma'am, who often threw things and broke things when she was unwillingly disturbed.

"Please, ma'am? Messages for you. Man call many times. He say very urgent."

With supreme effort, Claire swung her feet over the side of the bed. She glanced at herself in the mirror. Ouch. Reaching out for the messages, a sudden surge of nausea made her freeze momentarily. She muttered some words under her breath and waited a moment for the feeling to pass. The maid bowed her head lower, as if to avoid a blow.

Claire took the messages. She muttered thanks in Thai.

The little maid bowed deeply, then stood and started to shuffle backward out of the room.

"Make a bath for me!" Claire remembered to call, then winced as the words reverberated inside her pain-racked skull, making it feel like all the little blood vessels in her brain were leaking. "Please make a bath," Claire whispered again, adding the word *bath* in Thai.

Claire glanced at the first message. From Daedalus. She tossed it on the floor and looked at the second. Daedalus. Onto the floor. The third one read, *Get your ass to New Orleans, damn you.* She laughed and tossed it after its companions. The rest were just more of the same, just old Daedalus playing mayor, wanting an audience so he could pontificate about nothing, blah, blah, blah.

Claire reached over, found a bottle by the bed with a few inches of a pale yellow liquor in it. She took a swig, winced, and drew her sleeve across her mouth. Time to start the day.

I didn't remember getting back to Axelle's. The whole surreal day swam through my consciousness like bits of a movie I'd seen long ago. For six periods I'd dealt with stares and whispers, dealt with seeing Clio again and again as we passed each other in the hall, both of us jerking in renewed surprise. Thank God for Sylvie. In her I sensed a true friend—she treated me normally, helped me get my bearings, told me where classes were, how to meet her at lunch.

Clio was going to talk to her grandmother. So I had a grandmother too, for the first time in seventeen years. Doubt was pointless. It had been overwhelmingly obvious that Clio and I had once been one cell, split in two. Now that I knew I had an identical twin, I somehow felt twice as lost, twice as incomplete as before. Would that feeling go away if we became close? I had family now, real blood family, but I still felt so alone.

Dad hadn't known. I felt that instinctively. Never in any way had he ever revealed that he knew I'd been a twin. Which was a whole other mystery in itself.

I'd managed to get on the streetcar going downtown and got off at Canal Street, the end of the line. Like a trained dog, I found my way to Axelle's apartment. For just a minute I rested my forehead against the sun-warmed iron of the gate. *Please, please, let Axelle not be home. Or Daedalus or Jules. Please.*

I passed the small swimming pool in the courtyard and hesitated before I unlocked the door. How had Axelle gotten me? Who was she, really? Had she even known my dad? Because just as surely as I knew Clio was my sister, I also instinctively felt that I had been brought to New Orleans on purpose, and part of that purpose must be Clio. I paused for a moment, my key in my hand. Oh my God. Had Axelle caused my dad's death somehow? The timing was so . . . I took a deep breath and thought it through.

I didn't see how she could have done it. Remembering it was a fresh pain: my dad had been killed when an old woman had a stroke at the wheel of her car. It had jumped the curb and crashed through the drugstore window. My dad had been in the way. But the woman was from our town—old Mrs. Beadle. I'd known her by sight. There was no way Axelle could have bribed her. She'd broken her nose and her collarbone and gotten glass in one eye. Her driver's license had been taken away forever. Despite everything, even Mrs. Thompkins had felt sorry for her. No. Axelle and her gang of merry weirdos couldn't have had anything to do with it.

I opened the door and was met by a blast of air-conditioning, as usual. The air inside was stale with cigarettes but blessedly quiet and empty. In that instant, I knew no one was home, as if I could have felt the jangling energy their presence would make.

I dumped my backpack in my room and sat down on my bed, feeling numb. What was happening with my life? Even if Axelle hadn't caused my dad's death, still, it wasn't a coincidence that I had been brought halfway across America to a city I'd never been before only to run into my *identical twin*—the twin I never knew existed. Yet given how unconcerned Axelle had been about my going to school, I didn't see how meeting Clio today had been planned. If Axelle knew Clio was here, she hadn't planned on us meeting—at least not yet.

Restlessly I got up. She wasn't home, and I had no idea when she'd be back. I started roaming the apartment, deliberately snooping for the first time. My eyes fell on the door that led to the secret attic room. If anything was hidden in this apartment, it was in that room. I listened for Axelle. I heard nothing, felt nothing. There was a small brass knob right below the small brass lock. Could she have left it unlocked this once? I knew she carried the key with her.

I turned the doorknob and pulled.

Nothing happened. It was locked. Of course.

A wave of frustration made me grit my teeth. I needed answers! I closed my eyes, trying to calm the thousand questions swirling in my brain. I took some deep breaths. A lock, a lock . . . I was about to cry, as I hadn't all day, not since this morning when I'd gotten up. I pictured the lock in my mind. All I needed was a stupid key! I could see how the small key would slide into the lock, how its indentations would line up with the little row of pins in the cylinder....

I needed to think, to decide what to do. I leaned against the cool wall, my eyes closed, hand still on the knob. I reached my finger up and traced the keyhole. One stupid key. I would just put the key in, turn it, the pins would fall into place. . . . I could *see* it. I sighed heavily. Maybe I should go take a long tepid shower.

Then, under my finger, I imagined I felt the smallest of vibrations.

I opened my eyes. I listened. Silence. Stillness. I turned the doorknob and pulled gently.

The door opened.

I was in! Without hesitation I ran up the worn wooden steps. The plaster walls were decaying slightly, like everything else in New Orleans. Here and there bare brick was exposed.

I held my breath as I reached the door at the top of the stairs. God only knew what was behind here, and all of a sudden, horror-movie images filled my mind.

"Don't be ridiculous," I muttered, and turned the doorknob.

The door led to one dimly lit room, the only illumination coming from shuttered half-moon windows at either end. The ceiling was low, maybe eight feet in the center, and sloped down on both sides to maybe four feet. The air was completely still and the exact temperature of my skin. I could smell wood, incense, fire, and too many other intermingled scents for me to name. At one end was a scarred worktable that was covered with the same kinds of maps and plans and books I'd seen downstairs. At first glance, I saw no suitcase full of heroin, no huge opium pipes, as I'd feared. So it was just about the voodoo, then.

Low bookshelves lined the wall on one side, and, curious, I knelt to read their spines. Some of the titles were in French, but others read, *Candle-Burning Rituals for the Full Moon; Witch—A History; Astral Magick; Principles of Spellcraft; Magick, White and Black.*

I sat back on my heels. Oh, jeez. Magick. Witchcraft. Not a surprise, but a depressing confirmation. I looked around. The bare wooden floor had layers of dripped wax from candles. There were pale, smeared lines of circles within circles, all different sizes, around the candle wax. Other shelves held candles of all colors. An astrology chart was pinned to one crumbling wall. There were rows of glass jars, labeled in some other language— maybe French? Latin?

How incredibly asinine. It was like finding out they were Moonies. I couldn't believe anyone would spend so much time and energy and money on all this stuff. What idiots.

So the three of them did their "rites" up here. And that kid Richard too. God.

But . . . after my nightmare, Axelle had done spells in my room, like they would help protect me or something. Which meant she thought someone was trying to hurt me.

As if my nightmare had been witchcraft by someone else.

I suddenly felt dizzy, my head pounding. I had to get out of here this *second*. I ran to the door, raced down the steps, and pulled the door shut behind me. I heard a slight *snick*—it was locked again. Adrenaline raced through me, making my heart hammer, my breath come fast. I didn't even think of where to go but flew out of the apartment and out the side gate.

On the street I stopped short. It was still daylight, the sun intermittently covered with dark gray clouds. Tourists were walking by, as if nothing were unusual, as if my life hadn't changed hugely, not once, but too many times to count in the last month and today most of all. I slowed to a walk and crossed the narrow cobbled street. What to do, where to go—my thoughts weren't even that coherent. I just kept taking one step at a time, one foot in front of the other, feeling my skin film with cold sweat.

Then I found myself in front of the private garden, the garden where I'd met Luc.

Quickly I moved the ivy aside and pushed open the small wooden door. As soon as I was inside and the door shut behind me, I felt the cold dread start to leave me. Inside this quiet garden, I felt calmer, saner. Safe.

Once again I sank onto the marble bench, feeling its welcome coolness against my skin. I didn't want to search the windows of the surrounding buildings but hoped that Luc could see I was here. In a life filled with strangers, he and Sylvie were the only people I felt at ease with.

In the meantime I sat, letting my heartbeat slow, my breathing become regular. I couldn't think, couldn't begin to piece this puzzle together. I could only sit and listen to the muted sounds around me: the trickling fountain, the few small birds hopping among the jasmine, the very distant sounds of horses and carriages, tugboats on the river, streetcars rattling on their tracks.

I had a sister, a twin sister. I had a grandmother. Each time, I realized it all over again. Things with Clio had been strange. Maybe she didn't want a sister. Maybe she didn't want to share her grandmother—my grandmother. But surely my grandmother would want me? I closed my eyes and said a prayer that this was all real, that I had a real family now, that my grandmother would love me and take me to live with her, like in a fairy tale. *Please don't let me be alone anymore,* I prayed.

As before, I didn't hear the gate open, but when I looked up, Luc was walking toward me. A tight knot inside my chest eased, and all my tension started to evaporate. He was taller than I'd realized, wearing worn jeans and a white button-down shirt rolled back at the sleeves. A gentle smile lit his face, and it hit me again just how good-looking he was. And then I became aware of how grubby and dusty and hot I was, and my morning shower seemed a lifetime ago. Great.

"We meet again." He sat next to me on the bench, leaning forward to rest his arms on his knees. "You look upset. Again. Is your life so crazy right now?"

I gave a short laugh, wishing I had brushed my hair sometime in the last eight hours. "Yes."

He gave a sympathetic sigh, and it struck me how incredibly comforting he was to be with. He couldn't be more than a year or two older than me, but he seemed light-years away from most guys I'd known. I put my head to one side, thinking about it.

"What?" He smiled at me.

"I was just thinking. . . . You have a . . . deep stillness to you," I said. His eyes lost their dreamy expression, became more alert. "As if all of this"—I waved my hand to encompass the whole world—"washes over you without affecting you very much. You seem like a—" I paused, considering. "Like a tree in the middle of a river, kind of. And the river washes around you and past you, but the tree never moves." I laughed self-consciously at my description.

Luc didn't speak for a minute, just looked at me. "Is that how I seem to you?" he asked softly.

"Yes," I said, not caring if I sounded stupid. "Everything in my life has changed. It keeps changing every day. But when I sit here with you, it's like the world has stopped." I shrugged. "Like time has stopped. It's . . . peaceful. It makes me feel better. I can't explain it."

Luc leaned back against the vine-covered brick wall. I heard the sleepy hum of bees as they went from flower to flower among the Confederate jasmine. I remembered how Luc had told me the names of some of the

114

plants, and, leaning forward, I picked another perfect, creamy gardenia blossom. I inhaled its fragrance, its heady sweetness, and then I tucked it through a button-hole on his shirt pocket.

"One for you," I said, smiling.

Luc was very still, and now he looked at me with a slight, puzzled smile.

"What do you want from me, Thais?" he asked.

"What do I *want* from you?" I didn't understand.

"In relationships, people want things from each other," he explained, his voice patient. "Girls might want protection or someone to pay for things—someone to show off to their friends. Guys might want arm candy or someone to take care of them or just someone to sleep with. People are afraid to be alone, and so they cling to each other like flotsam after a shipwreck. So, what is it that you *want* from me? And also, what is it that you're *offering* me?" His crisply accented voice was very quiet, for my ears only in this still, private garden.

My mouth was hanging open. "Well, that was just about the most depressing, old-fashioned, sexist-pig view of relationships I've heard in a long time," I said. I felt hurt, as if he were implying that I wanted to use him somehow. "What rock have you been living under? How did you get so cynical this young?"

Luc cocked his head, studying me. His dark hair, his beautiful eyes, made me even madder because my strong attraction to his gorgeous outside was being spoiled by his dumb inside.

"And since when do we have a relationship?" I said, feeling anger rise in my veins. "We've run into each other *twice!*" My jaw set as I thought rapidly, already feeling the loss of something I hadn't even realized I wanted. "I am offering you *nothing*," I went on, practically spitting at him. "I'd rather stay alone the rest of my life than hook up with a guy who's only wondering what I *want* from him. And why would you even be worried? You *clearly* have nothing to offer *me*."

I pushed off from the bench and strode to the garden gate, furious at him for ruining everything when I'd felt so peaceful and calm. I'd reached out to yank the gate open when suddenly Luc grabbed my arm and swung me around. Emotion crossed his face: uncertainty, hope, and something I recognized at the last second as strong, intense wanting.

"You'd be surprised at what I can offer you," he said roughly, and then he was kissing me like Chad Woolcott had never kissed me in eight months of going out. Like no one had ever kissed me, ever. My head bent back over his arm and I felt the heat of his body through my clothes. It never occurred to me to resist, and I knew then that I'd wanted him all along. I felt the hardness of his arms holding me, pressing me to him. My eyes drifted shut, my mouth opened to his, and my arms wrapped around his neck as if I had no control over my own body. And maybe I didn't.

It felt like we kissed for ages, standing there, and finally we pulled away, as reluctantly as if pulling away meant death. Luc looked as shocked as I felt. I put my fingers to my lips—they felt bruised. Luc was breathing hard. He ran a hand through his dark hair and looked away.

All I could think was ... my world had just tilted. It was just a kiss, standing up, even, yet in that kiss it felt like everything in my life fell quietly into place and made sense.

Which it didn't, of course. My life was still a huge, thorny mess. But during that kiss I had been able to forget about it, forget about everything.

"I'm sorry," he muttered, looking completely unlike his usual cool, suave self.

"Don't be sorry," I whispered, trying to pull myself together. I glanced at the sky, almost dark, and then I felt the first heavy raindrop explode against my arm. My skin felt so hot I expected to see a little puff of steam. "I have to go." I didn't want to. I wanted to stay there forever.

He looked at me then, intensely, as if trying to see my soul. "We have a relationship," he said, and I got a weird feeling that he hadn't meant to say that, that it had come out anyway. "Even if I'm ... old-fashioned and sexist and cynical." He gave a short laugh.

"I'll be back," I said. And looking into his eyes, I saw my reflected knowledge that with one kiss, everything had spun out of control.

Clio

"Holy Mother," Racey breathed, looking at me. "I can't get over it."

I took the bag of Raisinets from her and got a small handful. "Me neither."

"So Petra knew about your mystery twin," she said.

I nodded. "She had to. She was stunned, but not surprised, if you know what I mean."

Racey nodded, leaning against my wall. It was getting late—soon she'd have to go. School night, etc. Like I could deal with school now. I could barely stand school when my life was somewhat normal—now it would be an unending agony.

"Well, oh my God," Racey said, trying to sound normal. She tucked her white-streaked hair behind one ear. "You told me you wanted a sister once."

"No. I said I wanted *you* to be my sister," I reminded her. "I don't want another *me* as a sister."

"That *would* be a nightmare," Racey agreed, and I kicked at her with my bare foot. She laughed and said, "So what's Petra's explanation, then?"

"Don't know," I said shortly. "Haven't heard it." I leaned against my headboard and pulled a pillow into my lap. "She said she'd explain it, but she started doing all these protection spells, and then later she said that she wanted to see Thais and me together."

"Do you think Thais'll come live here?"

I groaned. "I don't know. She's living with some friend of her dad's. But if Nan is an actual living relative . . . I mean, there's no room here! We'd have to share a room!" I kicked a pillow on the floor.

"Okay—it's a freak show," Racey agreed. "Got it. Let's talk about something else. How's the mysterious Andre?" She raised her eyebrows suggestively.

"How would I know?" I snarled. "I haven't seen him today because, oh, *yeah*, I found out that I had an identical twin sister that my grandmother has been lying to me about for seventeen years!"

Racey pursed her lips. "All *righty*, then. Who'd you get for chem lab?"

Unwillingly, trying to hold on to my outrage, I laughed. Only Racey could make me laugh at a time like this. "Foster."

"Me too! We can swap notes. Now, quick segue: so you still like Andre?"

"More than like. I mean, he's . . . he's just everything I could want." I shook my head. "He's perfect for me. I can't imagine ever wanting to be with anyone else."

Racey's eyes widened in alarm. She'd never heard me talk this way. I'd never heard me talk this way either. I'd been with tons of guys, and Andre was the first one who'd even gotten close to touching my heart. And he was more than close. This was all new territory for me. It was exciting. Kind of dangerous.

"Huh," she said, obviously thinking this through.

"Anyway: you and Jonah," I said. "What gives?" Racey and Jonah Weinberg had had a summer fling, and now he was in her English class.

"I may have underestimated him," Racey allowed.

I grinned. "He did look pretty good today, didn't he?"

"Yeah." She was about to elaborate when her cell phone rang. "Hey, Mom. Uh-huh. Yeah. Yeah, okay. Got it." She clicked the phone off. "It's a school night," she said brightly. "I better get my butt home so I can get a good night's sleep!"

I laughed, feeling better. "Okay. But thanks, Race. You're my lifeline." I hugged her.

"Clio—it'll be okay." She pulled back and looked into my eyes. "No matter what happens, it'll be okay, and I'll be here for you." We didn't usually get all sappy with each other, so I was touched.

"Thanks. And after all, *you* have sisters, right?" She had two sisters, both older, and Trey, just a year younger than us.

"Yeah." She frowned. "They suck." Then she pasted on a falsely enthusiastic face. "But I'm sure *your* sister will be *great!*"

I snorted and kicked her in the butt on the way out. *Thank you, Déesse, for friends.* It was the most heartfelt prayer I'd said all day.

Streetcars are not air-conditioned, like buses or subways. Instead they have windows that go up and down. Except for the window I was sitting next to, which was broken and wouldn't budge. I was already clammy and sticky, and it was barely eight thirty in the morning.

Axelle hadn't come home until almost ten o'clock last night. After I'd left Luc, I'd gone back and taken a long shower. When Axelle walked in, I was calmly eating a microwaved chicken potpie and going through my school papers at the table. So much for her wanting me to come straight home from school.

We hadn't talked much. I was dying to shriek questions at her: who was she, why was I here? But something held me back. Meeting Clio had made this whole scenario even stranger and more upsetting, and Axelle was a big part of it. Though she didn't actually seem dangerous, I was much more on my guard. Did she know about Clio? If she knew about Clio but hadn't mentioned her to me—then she didn't want me to know about her for some reason. So if I told Axelle that Clio went to my school, would she ever let me go back?

Or would this whole situation unravel horribly? So I just tried to act normal. Axelle was distracted and uninterested, and I slipped off to bed as soon as I could.

The next morning she'd still been sleeping when I left the house.

Now I sat on the swaying, clacking streetcar, leaning forward to catch the warm breeze from the open window by the seat in front of me. Once again I was nervous, on edge, as if Axelle would run up and pull me off the trolley. Or maybe a huge live oak would topple across the tracks and mash us. Or someone would try to snatch my backpack. Just something, some unnamed dread was weighing on me, winding me tight.

Maybe I should switch to decaf.

I was sitting toward the back—every seat was taken by people going to work, kids in Catholic school uniforms, kids going to École Bernardin and other schools.

When we passed Sacré Coeur, a Catholic girls' school, a lot of seats emptied. Still nervous, jumpy, I suddenly decided to move up front so I could see when École Bernardin appeared. I stood up, grabbed my backpack, and was three feet down the aisle when I heard someone scream. Time stretched out as I slowly turned.

Outside the back windows, a big, bright red pickup truck had jumped the curb and was flying toward the streetcar. I hardly had time to blink as the truck plowed into one of the old-fashioned streetlights that lined St. Charles Avenue. The streetlight snapped off a foot above the ground, and the top of it speared through the streetcar window, smashing the glass and reaching halfway across the aisle.

Right where I'd been sitting.

Streetcars can't stop on a dime, so we dragged the streetlight about twenty feet as the brakes screeched and shot sparks. I sank, weak-kneed, into the closest seat. If I hadn't moved, that broken, jagged streetlight would have speared me like a fish.

The driver strode toward the back of the streetcar.

"Anybody hurt?" he boomed, and we all looked at each other.

Despite the broken glass, no one had even a scratch. People had gotten almost knocked off their seats, but no one had fallen. It was amazing. I felt shaky, realizing what a close call I'd had.

"Okay, everybody move to the front of the car," the driver said authoritatively. "Watch out for the glass." He opened the back door of the streetcar and went onto the median, where a dazed teenager wearing a baseball cap was unfolding himself from the pickup.

The streetcar driver started yelling at the teenager, who looked scared and upset. I heard him moan, "My dad is gonna kill me."

"He's gonna haveta get in line!" the streetcar driver said angrily. "Look what you did to my trolley, fool!"

Then the police came. After they had checked everything out, that streetcar went out of service. I didn't want to wait for another one and walked the last ten blocks to school. The aftereffects of my near escape made me feel hyped up and anxious. Limp from humidity and damp with sweat, I got to school just after the first bell had rung.

A couple of people said hi—the whole twin story had probably made its rounds. I smiled shakily and said hi, grateful for any friendly face.

"Thais! Hey," said Sylvie, walking up. "Did you find your one-inch, three-ring binder with the clear panel outside for your name?" It had been on one of our supply lists.

I nodded and smiled faintly. "Yeah. But I just almost experienced death by light pole." I told her what had happened, trying not to sound as scared as I felt.

"Oh no!" she said sympathetically. "What a sucky way to start the morning. But I'm glad you're all right."

Sylvie liked me as me, not just as one of the bizarre separated twins. A thought of Luc popped into my mind—I wanted him to like me as me too. Granted, he didn't know about me and Clio. The image of our burning kiss seared my mind for just a moment, and I felt heat flush my cheeks.

"Yeah, it's already hot," Sylvie said as the second, tardy bell rang. "We better get to homeroom."

But as I turned, I saw Clio disappear into a room down the hall. For a second she met my eyes, and I tapped Sylvie's arm.

"You go ahead—I'm going to get a drink of water."

She nodded, and I took off down the hall, looking through glass doors. One room was unlit and empty and I almost passed it, but then I saw a dark silhouette. I opened the door and peered in.

"Clio?"

She was leaning against a desk, her long hair down around her shoulders. "Hey." She looked me up and down, as if to remind herself of how identical we were. She gestured to her right. "This is my . . . uh, nan. My grandmother. Nan, this is Thais."

An older woman stepped out of the shadows. I searched her face, but I'd definitely never seen her before. She didn't look like me or Clio or our mother.

"Thais," she said softly, stepping closer to me. She glanced from me to Clio and back. "My name is Petra Martin. You've . . . both . . . grown up beautifully. I'm so happy to finally see you again." Clio's grandmother. So my grandmother too. My mother's mother.

I'd never even known about her, and Clio had had her for seventeen years.

I swallowed nervously, hoping that she would want me too, that I had found my family. Quickly Petra hugged me. Her hair smelled like lavender.

She pulled back and smiled at me. "You've got to come with me now," she said, starting to walk to the outside door on the other side of the room.

Petra opened the door and headed briskly across the school yard to go off property. I hurried after her, and Clio followed me.

"Are we skipping out of school?" I had never done that in my life.

Petra gave me a quick glance, her eyes clear and blue and piercing. "Yes."

"Oh. Well." I nodded. "Okay." There's a first time for everything.

She led us to a Volvo station wagon, and five minutes later we pulled up in front of a small house, set back from the sidewalk and surrounded by one of the cast-iron fences I saw all over the place. The front garden was lush, so thickly planted that it practically concealed the house from the street. The house was small and painted a dark rust color, with natural wood trim. Two tall French windows opened onto the small porch, and the front door had stained glass around the main frosted pane. It was adorable.

After my dad had died, I'd felt more alone than I had thought possible. I'd practically wanted to die myself. Since I'd seen Clio yesterday, I'd been hoping and praying that somehow this would work out and the horrible, unbelievable turn my life had taken in the last couple months would be over. I wanted normalcy, a grandmother, a home, a sister. Real, normal people who would never take Dad's place, but be a close second.

The front door opened directly into a sparsely furnished living room. I looked around with interest, as if examining my new home. I wished.

The furniture was simple and old-fashioned. The walls were painted a dusty rose. I felt comfortable here— it was so much homier than Axelle's black-leather art deco stuff. Like in Axelle's main room, the ceilings were ridiculously tall, maybe twelve feet? Fourteen? Two wooden bookcases were centered on the far wall, and I read their titles, hoping they would give me clues as to what kind of person Petra was.

Crystal Working.

My breath caught in my throat as I hoped desperately that Petra was all into beading.

Wiccan Sabbats. Herbal Magick. Metal and Stone Work in Spells.

I couldn't keep the dismay off my face. All the hopes that had been born yesterday—my dreams for a real family, my sad need for a home and normalcy—withered inside me.

"You do voodoo," I muttered, blinking back tears. Then it hit me: Petra and Clio did this magick stuff—just like Axelle and the others. What were the chances of that? Just how common was it in New Orleans? I swallowed, feeling suddenly cold. Petra and Clio were my only family. Couldn't I trust them? Could I give them up, not have anything to do with them? I took a breath. I would hear Petra out. Then decide. Everything in me wanted Petra and Clio to belong to me and me to them. I would wait and see. If they were connected to Axelle somehow ...

"Not voodoo," said Petra with a little smile. "*Bonne Magie.* The Craft. Similar to Wicca, with the same roots. Now, come into the kitchen. We'll have tea."

The kitchen was painted a pretty green, and the two

windows both had shelves of healthy houseplants in front of them. A large white cat was asleep on top of some newspapers on the kitchen table. I felt crushed, devastated. I'd been so stupid to get my hopes up.

"Get the cat off the table," Petra said, going to the cupboard and taking out three glasses.

Clio picked up the cat and handed him to me. "This is Q-Tip."

I held him awkwardly. Q-Tip sleepily opened his blue eyes and looked at me. Then he closed his eyes and went heavily limp in my arms. For a moment I was surprised at how he'd accepted me, but then I realized I didn't look like a stranger.

"Q-Tip is a big boy," I murmured, looking around for a place to put him down. I didn't see one and finally just sat in a chair and arranged him on my lap. Petra put a tall glass of tea in front of me, and then the three of us were sitting there together. In a witch's house.

"He's deaf," Clio said as an icebreaker. "A lot of white, blue-eyed cats are."

"How do you call him?" I asked, trying to be polite.

Petra smiled, and suddenly her somewhat forbidding, stern-looking face relaxed and an affectionate warmth stunned me. I was still blinking in surprise when she said, "We stomp on the floor, hard enough to send vibrations through the house. Then he comes running. He comes even if he's outside, if he's close enough."

I looked down at the huge cat, impressed. He purred.

"Unfortunately, until just a few years ago, when Clio

was mad, she'd stamp her feet and slam doors," Petra went on wryly. Clio made a semi-embarrassed face across the table. "Finally she had to learn to get her temper under control, if only for the cat's sake."

"He kept running up, wanting treats," Clio admitted, and I smiled.

"Why do you do magick?" I blurted. "It seems so—"

"It's our family's religion, dear," Petra said, as if explaining why we were Lutherans. "What do you have against it?"

I realized I was on thin ice. Despite the magick, despite my worries about Axelle, I couldn't help wanting Petra to love me, to want me. I shrugged and drank my tea.

"I don't think I've ever stamped my foot or slammed a door," I said, returning to the earlier conversation. "Dad and I didn't fight much."

Petra's face softened when I mentioned my dad. "I'm very sorry you lost Michel, dear," she said gently. "I only met him once, but I thought he seemed very nice."

"If you met him, why didn't we both go with him?" I asked, and saw the same curiosity on Clio's face.

Petra sighed and took a deep drink of her tea. I was halfway through mine—it was unusual, not sweet, though I tasted traces of mint and honey. With surprise I realized that I felt unexpectedly comfortable, even relaxed.

"I'm going to tell you both what happened," Petra said, folding her fingers around her glass. "Yes, obviously, you're twins. Identical twins. And I was the one who separated you."

Clio

This oughta be good, I thought. Across the table, Thais had her gaze locked on Nan, and I wondered if the tea had kicked in yet. I could taste a trace of valerian and knew she'd brewed something to calm us all down, make this easier.

"I knew your mother, Clémence, was pregnant, of course, but she wasn't married and I didn't know who the father was until the night she came to me, in labor." Nan took a deep breath. "I'm a midwife, and Clémence wanted me to deliver her baby at home, not in a hospital," she explained to Thais.

"Why?" Thais asked.

"Because . . . she trusted me more than a hospital," Nan said slowly, as if reliving that time. "Because I'm a witch. As was Clémence."

I hid my smile behind taking a sip of tea. Thais sat back in her chair, looking, if possible, more horrified. I got up and put some cookies on the table. Numbly she reached out for one and took a distracted bite. I saw Q-Tip's ear twitch as she dropped crumbs on him.

"Witch how, exactly?" she asked, and I looked at her thoughtfully. She was bummed but not shocked. That was interesting.

"Our family's religion is called *Bonne Magie*," Petra said. "Good Magick, in English. White Magick, if you will. It's been our family's religion for hundreds of years—since about the sixth century. My ancestors brought it to Canada, then into America to Louisiana hundreds of years ago. But there's more to it than that."

Thais sipped her drink and absently stroked Q-Tip's fur. I wanted Nan to get to the part where she'd deprived me of my father. And deprived Thais of her grandmother, I admitted. If I thought of it that way, I couldn't help feeling I'd been the lucky one.

"Many people practice the Craft in different forms," Nan went on. "Wicca is a big example and the closest religion to what we have. *Bonne Magie* descended from the earliest forms of Wicca—the Celts brought it to Brittany when they came as refugees to escape the Anglo-Saxons."

I took a deep, impatient breath. *Cut to the chase.*

"Anyway," said Nan, "we and our ancestors have achieved something more. We've tapped into the deep magick contained within Nature herself. We have power."

Thais looked at her blankly. I'd grown up knowing all this, so it was like watching someone fold laundry. But to Thais it was all new, and I wondered what she was thinking.

"Uh-*huh*," she said, sounding like she was humoring a nutcase. Again I had to hide a smile. "Power."

Petra heard Thais's tone. "Yes, my dear, power. Power

and energy are contained within every natural thing on this planet, there to be tapped into, used, if you know how. Our religion is about knowing how, and even more important, knowing *why*."

Thais licked her lips and glanced sideways, as if plotting an escape route.

"Look," I said, pushing my glass away. I took the salt-cellar and dumped a small pile onto the table. I looked at it, then closed my eyes. I slowed my breathing and centered myself, then started singing softly under my breath. The basic form was in Old French, and it rhymed. I substituted a few words to make it apply to this situation.

> Salt of the earth
> Power of life
> I shape you
> I make you mine
> We become one.

I pictured the tiny, individual salt grains. I let my energy flow out and around them so it was like I had no boundaries in my body anymore. I was part of everything, and because I was part of everything, I could affect everything.

A minute later I opened my eyes. Thais looked like someone had just smacked her upside the head. She stared at the table, then up at me. She scooted her chair back, leaned over Q-Tip, and looked beneath the table for hidden wires or magnets.

"It's just salt," I told her. "It's not, like, metal shavings. Not a lot can affect it. Except magick."

She looked at the table again, where a round happy face made of salt smiled at her.

"Of course," Petra said dryly, "magick also has larger, more important purposes. But that was just one small demonstration of what we call power. I don't think Michel knew your mother was a witch. He himself was not. And I tell you all this to set the stage, to help explain why I acted as I did."

"Our family can trace its line back more than a century," Nan said. "And since the very beginning, it's had an issue with twins."

"What?" I'd never heard that before. "*An issue?*"

"Yes," Nan said. "In our line, twins are special because they can join their magick to become very powerful—much more powerful than any other two people using their magick together. Identical twins who know what they're doing can have a great deal of power indeed." Nan met my eyes, then Thais's. "Even a dangerous amount of power."

This was the most interesting thing I'd heard in ages. I looked at Thais speculatively, wondering how long it would take to get her up to speed magick-wise.

"So people in our line fear twins," Nan went on, and I frowned. "More than once, a set of identical twins has used their combined power not for good, but for dark purposes. They caused destruction, disaster, and death. The most recent time was about two hundred years ago."

"Were they crazy, to use it for evil?" I asked. Seeing Thais's face, I explained, "Any magick you put out into the world comes back to you threefold. So anyone with half a brain is careful to use their force only for good. Anyone who uses magick for a dark purpose is risking having hellfire come down on them."

"Yes," Nan agreed. "And hellfire did come down on them, their families, their communities, with disastrous consequences. This happened not only once, but at least three times in our history. So even today, in the twenty-first century, our people are wary of twins. More than wary—afraid. And fear makes people dangerous. When your mother gave birth that night, almost eighteen years ago, to twins, identical girls, I instantly knew that you would face prejudice, fear, persecution, and even danger from people afraid of you."

"But—I mean, how many of you are there? Why couldn't we have just moved someplace else and grown up normally? How many people would even know about us and would care enough to actually try to hurt us?" Thais shook her head. "I still don't get it."

"Of people who practice *Bonne Magie*, of course it's hard to know an exact number," said Nan. "I believe there are roughly twenty thousand or so. Maybe six thousand in America, more in France and other parts of Europe. Maybe eight thousand in Canada."

"That still doesn't seem like that many," Thais argued. "There're two hundred and ninety-five million people in America."

"Comparatively, it's not," Nan agreed. "But you don't need huge numbers for a group of people to wield a great deal of influence and for their powers to stretch over far distances. Our particular *famille*, with less than a thousand hereditary witches, all grew up with the cultural fear of our kind having twins."

"So you split us up," I said. "Voilà, no more twins."

"Did my dad know?" Thais asked.

Nan seemed uncomfortable. She shook her head, looking sad, remembering. "Your mother knew, of course. That's another reason she came to me. She was afraid for you, even before you were born. She kept you a secret from everyone, even me, even your father, until the night she had you. That night, she begged me to keep you safe. Thais, you were born just before midnight, and Clio, you were born just after midnight. That's why you have different birth dates. And then, with her dying breath, Clémence made me promise to do everything within my power to keep you safe."

Thais's eyes were brimming with tears. Seeing that made my own eyes fill.

Nan went on. "When I found out that Michel didn't know there was more than one baby, I didn't know what to do. Then—something went wrong during the delivery. Even if Clémence had been in a hospital, nothing could have saved her. It all happened so fast. But she had a minute, and she knew she was dying, and she begged me to save her daughters."

Nan cleared her throat and took a sip of tea. Thais's tears were running down her cheeks. I wiped my own eyes and swallowed the lump in my throat.

"I had no time to think." Nan took a strand of hair and tucked it back into her long braid. "Michel was waiting in the next room. Clémence had just died, and I would have to call the police, the hospital." I couldn't even imagine what that night had been like for her.

"And I had these two infants, wrapped in blankets," Nan said. "So I hid one, and I called Michel in and placed the other in his arms. In that one instant, he gained a daughter and lost his lover. I never mentioned the other baby or the twin curse. I told him where to take the baby for her to be checked out. I told him where they would take Clémence and about the arrangements he would need to make. He was shocked and heartbroken, and never have I felt sorrier for any human being than I did that night for Michel, holding his daughter, mourning his lost love."

Now I was crying too, for the young parents I had never known, for how painful it must have been for Nan, for myself, losing a mother, father, and sister all in one night. And for Thais, because she had lost her mother, grandmother, and sister in one stroke too.

"That was in Boston," said Nan. "Within a week, I had closed my midwifery practice and moved with Clio to New Orleans." She put her hand on mine. "I had a birth certificate made for you, and then you were mine. And though it absolutely broke my heart in two, I didn't leave my forwarding address with Michel, and I threw his information away. I didn't want to take any chances that one of our *famille* would discover you and perhaps make their own plans for ensuring that you never have a chance to wreak your powers of destruction."

"But then why am I here?" Thais cried, her voice broken with tears. "What's happened?"

"Obviously someone has found out," said Nan, an edge of steel underlying her calm voice. "Which leads me to ask: how did your father die, and who do you live with now?"

Thais blinked, trying to gather her thoughts. "Uh, Dad died in an accident," she said, taking a tissue from the box on the table. "He got hit by a car that jumped the curb." For a moment she frowned, thinking, as if something was just occurring to her, but then her face cleared and she went on. "Then in court I thought I was going to go live with Mrs. Thompkins, who was our best friend, like a grandmother to me. But Dad's will gave me to an old friend of his, who I'd never even heard of."

"*Who?*" Nan said, her fingers tightening around her glass.

"Her name is Axelle Gauvin," Thais said, and Nan's glass tipped, spilling tea. I saw Thais's eyes narrow slightly as I jumped up to get a dish towel. Tea and ice had spilled on Q-Tip, and he leaped down in disgust and trotted into the other room.

"So I take it you've heard of Axelle Gauvin?" I said dryly as I moped up spilled tea.

"Yes," Nan said grimly. "She's from our line, our original line. Her ancestors and mine were in the same *famille*."

"She's a relative?" Thais asked intently.

"Not by blood," Nan said. "It's more like a clan. Many people came here from Canada, of course. Many of them are now called Cajuns. But our particular group had fifteen families. Clearly, Axelle knows about you and Clio. She's brought you here for a reason."

Thais looked stricken. "That's what I've been worried about. How did she know when my dad died? How did she get to have me? And then both of you do magick—" Thais's chin trembled. "Oh God," she said faintly, sounding near tears. "Did she kill my dad?"

"Axelle is a lot of things, but a murderer? I have to say I don't think she could do it," said Nan firmly. "You've been safe with her this far. No one's tried to harm you, have they?"

Thais frowned, thinking. "Not really, no." She shook her head. "Do you know Jules and Daedalus too?"

Nan nodded.

"They're over at Axelle's a lot," said Thais. "They're a little creepy, but no one's ever tried to hurt me. In her own way, Axelle seems kind of concerned about me. She gave me a cell phone. Oh, and one night—I had a bad dream. Axelle did spells in my room after that."

For several minutes we sat there, each of us lost in thought. This was a lot of stuff to take in. Now I understood why Nan had freaked about Thais and why she'd put all the protection spells on the house and yard. I wondered if I had to go back to school today and if there was any way I could sneak over to see Andre instead.

"I think for now, it's safe for you to stay at Axelle's," Nan decided. "I'll talk to her, and then we should consider your living here."

Thais's face lit up just as I felt mine shut down. There was no room here for Thais. I mean, she was okay, and she was my sister, but this was all happening too fast.

"But for right now, stay at Axelle's. Keep your eyes and ears open; be extra careful, extra cautious," said Nan. "And I also think it would be safer if you started learning some magick. It would help you protect yourself."

"Uh . . ." Thais looked less than thrilled at this idea.

"Now I'm going to take you both back to school," said Nan. "I'll write notes so you won't have any trouble. Clio, you come straight home after school, and Thais, you go straight to Axelle's, understand?"

I somehow avoided making a face. I would run home after school, drop off my books, change, and go see Andre.

Then Nan hugged me and Thais in turn. "Despite everything, I am very glad to have you two reunited again. I'm so happy to see both of you at once, to know both of you. We're a family, and once we get this sorted out, it will all seem much better."

"What?" I whispered.

Sylvie gave an embarrassed smile and propped her workbook up so the study hall monitor wouldn't see us talking. "Sorry. I don't mean to stare. It's just—I've known Clio for three years, and now I know you, and you guys are so different. I mean, I was never good friends with Clio or anything. But still, you *look* so much alike, but you're really nothing alike."

"We dress differently," I said. Being back at school after my X-Files morning was weird, but school felt safer and more familiar than the rest of my life.

"It's more than that," Sylvie said. "You're just really *nice.*"

I winced. "Ouch."

She grinned. "Not goody-goody nice. But not a user, you know? I'm not saying Clio's mean, exactly. She's never been mean to me. But she's always been one of the really popular girls. Girls want to be her, and guys want to date her, and she knows it. And she gets into it." Sylvie stopped, as if she'd just realized she was talking about my sister and didn't want to hurt my feelings.

I thought about my life back in Welsford. I had been

one of the popular girls, and guys had asked me out. I knew people had thought I was pretty. In a way, I hadn't known how pretty I was until I had seen Clio. I saw her and how people reacted to her, and I realized they would react to me that way too. Was that what Luc saw? I thought again of his kiss for the nine-millionth time that day. Even at Petra's, hearing about my family's unbelievable past, I had thought of him again and again. What would happen the next time I saw him? Was I ready for it?

"What are you thinking about?" Sylvie asked behind her hand.

"Oh—just, back home, you know," I said, putting Luc out of my mind before I blushed. "It was so different than it is here. My school was really small, and we'd all started together in kindergarten, and no one was all that much better or worse than anyone else. So being pretty or popular didn't really get you anywhere." École Bernardin was about ten times bigger than my last school had been, and even on my second day I could see clear tiers of social strata. Clio and her friends were at the top.

I wondered where I would end up.

Axelle was waiting for me at the door of the apartment, pacing and smoking. I came in and our eyes met, a world of knowledge passing between us.

"Petra called me," she said.

I walked past her and dumped my backpack in my

room, then came out into the kitchen and poured myself a glass of seltzer. Finally, practically trembling, I faced her. Despite what Petra had said, I had to ask Axelle myself.

"Did you kill my father?" My voice was like ice. I'd never heard it sound like that.

"No." Axelle frowned. "I didn't even know him."

"Then how did I end up with you?" I yelled, taking us both by surprise.

Axelle looked defensive. "We . . . kept in touch with your father because of Clémence," she said. "When he died . . . unexpectedly, we thought it would be best if you came here, where you have people in your *famille*. I admit I pulled a few strings after your father died. It was important that I get you here. And really, don't you agree it's in your best interest? Aren't you glad you met your sister? And your . . . grandmother?"

"Of course," I said with gritted teeth. "But you did all this behind my back. And if I hadn't run into Clio at school, I still wouldn't know about my sister and grandmother. When were you planning to tell me?"

Axelle took a moment. I could practically see the mental gears turning. "The less you know, the safer it is for you," she said. "Of course I would have told you—when the time was right. You just found out a little sooner is all. Eventually, everything will be clear."

"So you're a witch too?"

"Of course," said Axelle. "Just as you are."

I ignored that. "You're part of the same *famille* as

Petra?" I tried to pronounce the French word as I'd heard Petra say it.

Axelle looked at me consideringly, her black eyes thoughtful. "Yes. The same as you."

"What about Jules and Daedalus?"

"Yes."

"Even that kid Richard, the goth guy? He's a witch?"

"Yes."

"Petra knows all of you?"

Axelle nodded.

"And you've always known Clio?"

"No. I saw her once, from a distance. But none of us know her, and she doesn't actually know any of us."

"So what's going to happen now?" I crossed my arms over my chest and stared at her.

Axelle's face seemed to close, and it was like I could actually see emotions shutting down. "Nothing. Business as usual. No huge fireworks or anything. Listen, I'm going upstairs for a while. Later we'll order in Chinese." She turned on her spiked heel and went into the main room. I heard the door open and then the click of her sandals on the wooden steps. She didn't know I'd been up there. I had my secrets too.

An image of Luc flitted through my thoughts, and I got up to go to the garden. But just as I opened the front door, a thunderstorm blew in from out of nowhere. I'd gotten used to this happening almost every day, sometimes twice a day. One minute it was sunny, the next it would be literally black outside, with rain falling so hard and thick that you literally couldn't see through it. Not even Connecticut nor'easters came close to a regular New Orleans summer storm.

Inside the apartment it was dark and cool. Outside it was pouring, with lightning and thunder. I sighed. We'd probably lose power soon. Since I'd lived here, we'd lost power maybe five times already. Just for a few minutes or an hour, but it was still disconcerting to have everything suddenly shut down.

An instantaneous *boom!* of thunder and a blinding flash of lightning that made the courtyard glow made up my mind for me. I closed the door. Back in my room I lay on my bed, listening to the buckets of rain drumming on the low roof over me. It was oddly soothing, comforting, and despite thunder that reverberated inside my chest and lightning that made the world go white, I actually fell asleep.

We Have a Full Treize

Ouida Jeffers parked her small rental car in a pay lot and walked the last two blocks to Daedalus's rented apartment. The heavy rain had stopped, and now thin curtains of steam rose from the cobbled streets. She didn't know how he could stand the French Quarter. It was always loud, always crowded, and there was no place to park. Years ago it had been lovely, much less touristy, more charming and authentic. But that had been a long time ago.

Ouida double-checked the apartment number and rang the bell.

"Yes?" a voice called from the upstairs balcony, and Ouida backed up into the street so he could see her. "Ouida!" said Jules, pleasure lighting his face. "I'll buzz you up!"

Ouida pushed the door when it buzzed and walked up the beautiful, floating staircase that curved around the courtyard to the second story. Jules had looked strained, she thought. He often did. He put so much pressure on himself.

As Ouida reached the landing, a tall wooden door opened, and Jules came out to hug her.

"Long time, old friend," he said, and she nodded into his shoulder. "I'm glad you're here."

"What's going on?" Ouida said in a low voice, but Jules didn't answer, just led her into the front parlor. Ouida looked around. Daedalus had always had impeccable taste. This apartment's balconies overlooked Chartres Street, with huge Boston ferns shielding the view a bit. Inside, graceful Empire furniture created an elegant, old-fashioned ambience. The whole effect was light, airy, and whispered old money.

"Ouida." Daedalus came forward, holding out his hands. They kissed formally on both cheeks and looked at each other. *We always do this*, Ouida thought. *When we see other members of the Treize, we examine them like medical curiosities.*

"How nice to see you, my dear," Daedalus said. "Come in, make yourself comfortable."

Ouida sank onto a delicate love seat. It had been hectic and difficult to arrange to come here. Fortunately, her research project could be put on hold, at least for a while. The chromosome samples weren't going anywhere. Daedalus had never summoned her like this, and she was curious.

"What's going on, Daedalus?" she asked as he handed her a tall, cold drink.

"You won't believe it," he said with a smile, sitting down opposite her. Jules sat down also. He didn't look nearly as cheerful as Daedalus did.

Ouida waited. Daedalus had always been a showman. Now he leaned forward, his blue eyes bright, energetic. "We can do the rite. We have a full Treize once more."

"Wh . . ." Ouida began, but her voice failed her. She looked quickly from Daedalus to Jules, and Jules nodded in confirmation. The breath had left her lungs, and now she tried to get enough air to speak. "What do you mean? Surely Melita—"

Daedalus waved his hand impatiently. "God, no. I have no idea where Melita is. As far as anyone can tell, she was swallowed up by the earth right after she left. But now, at last, we have a full thirteen. Thirteen witches of the *famille* to perform the rite."

"How? Who?" Ouida asked. Emotions she hadn't felt in years flooded her brain. Memories, yearnings, things that happened so long ago it was as if they'd happened to a completely different person.

"Twins," said Daedalus with great satisfaction. "From Cerise's line. Identical female twins."

"Twins? Where are they?" Ouida asked, so taken aback her head was swimming.

"Here, in New Orleans," said Jules. "It turns out Petra's had one for the last seventeen years. And then last summer, Daedalus and I found the other. Quite by chance."

Ouida frowned, thinking. "I saw Clio when she was a little girl. But she wasn't a twin."

"Turns out she was," Jules said. "Petra had divided them and hidden one."

"To prevent this from happening." Ouida under-stood immediately.

"Yes," Daedalus admitted. "But it isn't only Petra's decision. It affects all of us. It's something we've always wanted."

"Ouida."

Ouida turned to see the voice's owner. Her eyes met Richard's intensely, and for a moment everything was quiet. Then she rose and went to him. Ouida was barely five-foot two, and her head fit neatly into Richard's shoulder. They hugged for a long time until Richard drew back and smiled at her. "How was your flight?"

"It sucked," she said, smiling back. He knew she hated flying. She looked at his pierced eyebrow—that was new. He could get away with something like that, where it would look ridiculous on Jules or Daedalus. "You look very . . . young," she said, and he laughed.

"Love you, babe," he said, and went to pour himself a drink.

"So, these twins theoretically complete the thirteen," Ouida said, sitting back down. "But what about the actual rest of the Treize?"

"Petra is here, of course," said Daedalus, his eyes on Richard as he went to sit next to Ouida. "We haven't hashed out all the details—and I for one feel that she owes us a serious accounting of why she took matters into her own hands. Not telling us? Hiding a twin? She's done us all a great disservice. At best. But she's still one of us in the end, and I assume she won't let us down.

Sophie and Manon are arriving tomorrow, I believe. Everyone is coming."

Ouida looked at Daedalus knowingly. He was assuming a lot, and not only about Petra. "Everyone?" she questioned.

Daedalus shrugged. "We might have a few hitches. But everyone will be here soon."

Richard put his head back and tossed a pecan in the air, catching it expertly in his mouth. "Yeah. A few hitches. That's one way to put it."

"Claire?" Ouida asked, and Daedalus's face gave her the answer. "And . . . Marcel?"

Daedalus made an impatient gesture. "They will come."

Richard met Ouida's eye. Clearly he was skeptical that Daedalus could get the last two members here. Ouida suddenly felt very tired. She leaned back against the heavy silk upholstery. "It isn't just the Treize," she said. "There are so many other factors."

"All of which we've been working on," Daedalus said smoothly. "Everything is well under control. It could even happen by *Recolte*. But more likely by *Monvoile*."

Ouida found this all so hard to believe. After all this time, was this even what they wanted? Clearly Daedalus did. And Jules. But Richard? She looked at his young face. He looked back at her, and she found it hard to read his expression.

Abruptly she got up and put her glass on the table. "Well, this was certainly unexpected," she said. "It's a lot to think about. Right now I'm going to my B & B and sleep for a day."

Daedalus's eyes followed her. "Certainly, my dear. Rest. I know this is a lot to take in. Jules and I have had several months to absorb its implications. I know we'll be able to count on you when the time comes."

Ouida looked at him and didn't reply. She picked up her purse and walked to the door. "I'll be in touch." She let herself out, feeling three pairs of speculative eyes on her back.

Salvation Being Snatched Away

Sleep eluded him. Marcel turned restlessly on his pallet, its straw rustling with every movement. In truth, he dreaded sleep. In his sleep he was prey to dreams. Awake, he was prey to Daedalus. Today he had served as an acolyte at mass. As he'd lit the tall altar candle, young Sean, sent up from the village to assist here and there, had turned to him and said, "Come to New Orleans." Startled, Marcel had almost dropped his tall taper. He'd seen the blankness in Sean's eyes and realized the boy had no memory of having spoken.

So waking hours were unbearably tense. And sleep—the dreams that twisted through his mind, making him wake sobbing, tears running down his face ...

Death would be such a sweet release.

If only, if only ...

The small cell he'd occupied for the last five years had become such a refuge for him. He'd almost become hopeful, as his days blended into one another, the seasons flowing through his hands like rain. He worked hard, studied hard, prayed with the fervor of the converted. And now, after everything, it was being taken away from him. His hope, his peace, his possible salvation, all being snatched away by Daedalus. And for what?

Marcel turned again, his face to the stone wall. From a foot away he felt the chill wafting off the stones and he closed his eyes. His single candle had guttered and gone out hours ago. Soon it would be time for matins, and he would have passed the brief night with no sleep. Through the one small, high window, he had seen the sliver of moon arc across the sky and disappear from view.

Then it was there with no warning: Marcel was once again standing in a circle before the huge cypress tree. Melita was beginning the incantation. He could see everyone's faces: Daedalus, watchful, intrigued; Jules, frightened, unable to move; Ouida, curious; Manon, excited, like the child she was. Himself. Curious, eager, yet with a dark weight on his chest: fear.

The storm, the crack of lightning. The white glow on everyone's faces, sending their features into sharp relief, like a frieze. He saw Cerise, her face young and open, her belly heavy and round. The child not due for almost two months. Then the blast of power, striking them all like a fist. His mind clasping the energy like a snake, writhing within him. The exaltation ... the unbelievable power, the fierce, proud hunger they all felt, tasting that power. The gurgling spring, bubbling up from the ground, dark, like blood. Then the lightning flashed and they saw it *was* blood, and Cerise was holding her belly, her face twisting in pain. The blood around her ankles, Petra springing to her side, Richard's face so young and white ...

Marcel hadn't moved, had watched everything in a stupor, still drunk with the power that flowed through him.

Cerise had died as everyone crowded around her. Everyone except him and Melita. Melita had also been reveling in the power, had glanced across at him with a supremely victorious expression. The power lit her in glory, and she felt only an exquisite joy so sharp it bordered on pain. He saw that, saw Melita's face, as her younger sister died in childbirth on the ground.

Petra had held up the bloody, wriggling infant, small and weak, but mewling, alive.

"Whose child is this?" she had called, her voice barely audible over the pouring rain that was already washing Cerise's body clean. "Whose child is this?"

No one had answered. Cerise had died without revealing the name of her child's father.

But Marcel had known.

Now, in his cell, he was jarred by the deep, pealing sound of the bells announcing matins, calling the faithful to morning prayer. It was still dark outside. Automatically, Marcel rose and walked to the chipped metal basin that stood on a rough table. He splashed icy water on his face. The water mingled with his tears and left his face flushed and tingling.

Moving as if drawn by invisible thread, Marcel plodded silently down the dark stone hall. Time to pray for his soul once again. To beg for mercy from the all-merciful Father.

It would do no good.

"I can't believe Petra let you out," Racey said under her breath. Of all my friends, Racey was the only one I'd told about the whole curse-of-the-twins thing. Everyone else just thought that Nan had somehow, tragically, lost track of Thais and her dad until now. Now we were going to be one big happy and so on.

Ahead of us, Eugenie and Della were laughing, their high-heeled slides tapping against the sidewalk. We'd left Racey's mom's car down on Rue Burgundy—parking close to Amadeo's was impossible. It was only a few blocks, anyway.

"I'm in a group," I pointed out, giving Racey the same rationale I'd given Nan. "And I have to be back by eleven."

Racey grimaced, and I nodded glumly. "I told her I *needed* to go out and have a good time, not worry about anything," I said. "This whole thing has totally freaked me out. I can't think about it right now. But I have to be really careful, stay with you guys, yada yada yada."

Racey sighed sympathetically. "Did you get ahold of Andre?"

"I left a message—hope he gets it," I said. "I'm dying to see him." To put it mildly. It felt like a year since we had lain together under the oak tree in the park. That had been the last time I'd felt normal or at ease, and I was desperate to feel that way again, desperate to see the one person who made me forget about everything else that was happening.

"So Della's hot for Collier Collier," Eugenie called back over her shoulder, and Della whapped her on the shoulder.

My eyebrows rose. "The *sophomore?*"

Della looked embarrassed as Racey and I caught up with them. "He's a really hot sophomore," she defended herself. As if to change the subject, she gestured at a shortcut, a small alley that would let us skip two tourist-clogged blocks. We turned down it.

I thought about Collier Collier. "Yeah, in a young, contributing-to-the-delinquency-of-a-minor kind of way," I said. "He's what, fifteen? And you're going to be eighteen, when? Next week?" This alley was narrow and unlit, but I could already see the light and noise of Royal Street ahead of us.

"He's *almost* sixteen, and I won't be eighteen till next *April*," Della said. "There's not that huge a difference. And I mean, God. He's gorgeous."

Actually, he *was* gorgeous, which was the only reason I knew the name of a sophomore.

"I noticed him last year," Della admitted. "Remember? He was almost pretty. But over the summer, he grew, like, five inches—"

"Let's hope in the right place," Eugenie murmured, and I laughed out loud.

Della whapped her again on the arm. "And he's just really, really hot."

"Plus, he's a lowly sophomore, and you're a hot senior babe, and he's going to follow you around like a puppy," Racey said dryly.

"He *has* been very agreeable," Della said innocently.

"And pathetically grateful?" I asked.

"Don't know yet," Della said with a wicked smile. "But I assume so."

I was laughing again, but it suddenly choked off. Alarm flashed through me, but from what? I looked at Racey quickly, and she frowned. Then her eyes widened and she looked around—

"Gimme your wallets!" He stepped out of the shadows so fast that Eugenie squeaked and tottered on her heels. The guy had a knife and looked rough, unshaven, with torn clothes and a wild expression in his eyes. I cast my senses out—he wasn't a witch, which was why I hadn't picked up on him till it was too late.

I held up my hands. "Okay, okay," I said tensely. My heart was hammering in my chest, and I felt jittery with fear.

"Shut up! Gimme your wallet, bitch!" he snarled again, looking at me, and my throat closed even as my brain kicked into high gear.

We all fumbled for our purses. Eugenie was visibly

shaking and accidentally tipped hers out so everything spilled to the ground.

"Damn it!" she hissed, sounding near tears.

"It's okay," I said again, trying to sound calm. "Just pick your stuff up, Eu. Look, I'm taking out my wallet. . . ."

Everything happened so fast after that. For no reason, the guy suddenly freaked out and tried to backhand me across the face. I managed to jump back in time, and I saw Racey make a quick motion. The guy blinked, confused for a second, and I snapped my hand out and shot a bolt of *fourjet* at him.

He reeled as if he'd been punched on the shoulder, but then his crazed, bloodshot eyes fastened on me again, and he lunged at me with his knife. The blade whipped close enough for me to feel its *swish*, but I leaped to one side and sent another bolt of *fourjet* at his knees, which promptly buckled.

Looking surprised, he dropped to his knees, and then Della snarled in rage and swung her purse at his head as hard as she could. Della carries *everything* in her purse—I'd picked it up once and said, "What do you have in here? Bricks?"

It cracked against the mugger's head just as I whispered a *sortilège d'attacher*—a binding spell—feeling grateful that Nan had made me practice them until I wept with fatigue. The mugger went over sideways, looking stunned. I flicked my wrist and knocked his knife away, then shot it over and down a drain I saw out of the corner of my eye. Racey stood over him, silently adding her spells to mine to hold him in place.

He started howling, swearing, calling us names as he struggled futilely against the invisible bonds. Racey made a tiny gesture and then even his voice went mute. His eyes bugged out of his head in fear, and the four of us started backing away.

"What did you do, Della?" Eugenie cried.

"Maybe he's epileptic," Della said, sounding scared.

At that moment I saw a tall, dark figure enter the alley and start running toward us.

"Guys, run!" I cried, grabbing Eugenie's arm. "He had a partner!" We turned and raced for the other end of the alley, which would take us out into the crowded light of Royal Street. We were almost out when I heard my name being called.

"Clio! Clio, wait!"

I screeched to a halt. "It's Andre!" I whirled and peered down the dark alley.

Andre ran right past the mugger, barely glancing down at him. We waited at the end of the alley, in clear view of everyone passing on the street. Andre caught up to us and grabbed my arms. "Are you okay? I was half a block behind you. Didn't you hear me calling you?"

"No," I said, looking past him. The mugger was still lying on the ground. I could feel his helpless rage from here. "That guy tried to mug us!"

Andre swore under his breath, looking angry. Della

and Eugenie hadn't met him yet, and despite the shaky aftermath of almost being mugged, they were looking at him, impressed.

"I tried to catch up to you," Andre said. "That alley was *not* a good idea."

I saw a beat policeman strolling down the street, and I ran to catch up to him. "Um, a guy fell down in that alley back there," I said, pointing. "Maybe he's having an epileptic fit." The cop started walking quickly toward the alley, reaching for his walkie-talkie. I debated telling him that the guy had tried to mug us, but the cop was going to have a hard time dealing with the binding spells as it was. I didn't want to give an official statement or have to explain anything.

"That cop is going to go check on him," I told everyone.

"Should we report what he did?" Della asked. "If I do and my parents find out—"

"Me too," said Eugenie. "Goodbye, Quarter."

"Let's get out of here," I said. "The cop will take care of it. I just want to sit down."

We had walked quickly down half a block before I remembered to introduce Della and Eugenie to Andre. He smiled at them, and I could see his magic working on them. Not real magick, of course—just his own personal attraction.

We turned into Amadeo's, where it was blessedly dark after the overlit street. The bouncer let Andre in but wanted to card us. I sent him a "we're of age, don't

159

worry about it" thought, and he waved us through, looking bored.

"Friend of yours?" Andre said, nodding at the bouncer. He knew I was still in high school.

I shrugged. "Something like that. Hey, what about you? You're what, nineteen?"

Andre grinned, looking dark and mysterious. "Fake ID."

We got drinks and went to the back room. A live band was going to start soon since it was Friday, but we found a small empty couch and pulled some chairs over to it. Again I felt that Racey was watching Andre, as if trying to figure him out. Then she seemed to shake off the feeling and put a smile on her face. I saw her make eye contact with a guy sitting at another table, and soon they had a flirtation going. Within minutes Della and Eugenie had drifted off to check out guys, leaving Andre and me alone.

"Are you all right?" he asked, getting closer and putting his arm around my shoulders. "I practically felt my heart stop when I saw you duck down that alley. I've only been here two months, but even I know that you never go down a dark alley in New Orleans."

A delayed reaction to the mugging suddenly came over me, and I shivered and scooted closer to him. "I know," I said. "We weren't thinking—we were teasing Della about something and she just pointed to the alley and we went down it without paying attention.

And I've taken that shortcut a million times—just not at night."

Andre pressed a kiss into my hair. "How did you get away from him? I saw him drop, and then you started running."

What would I say? Racey and I were witches and we zapped him with spells? I didn't think so. "Della hit him with her purse," I said, smiling at the memory. "He went down like an ox. She carries, like, lead weights in there."

Andre laughed. "He's sorry he messed with you, no doubt."

I nodded, starting to feel smug about how we had dealt with that scumbag. "He'll think twice before he picks on lone girls again."

I looked into Andre's eyes, and my smile faded. I could get lost in his eyes so quickly, so totally. I reached out and touched his lips softly. "I'm glad you got my message to meet us here," I said. "I missed you yesterday."

"What happened? I was hoping to see you."

I hesitated. Oh, my whole world changed, that's all. Suddenly explaining everything to Andre—Thais, my past—it was all too much. I needed to figure out a way to tell him without mentioning all the witch stuff. Someday he could know everything. Someday soon. But not tonight. "School, and then Nan needed me at home."

"Everything okay?" he asked, smoothing my hair away from my face. His finger traced down my cheek, then my neck, past my collarbone. It dipped slightly under my lacy black camisole, and I shivered again, but not with fear.

I shrugged. "Just family stuff." Huge, bizarre family stuff. I spread my hands on his hard, warm shoulders and smiled flirtatiously at him. "When can we be alone?"

Sharp interest lit his eyes, and he gave me a predatory look that made butterfly wings feather lightly inside my chest. I was usually the predator with guys. Sometimes I let them pretend to be the one who pounced, but really, it was always me. Which was how I liked it.

Now, with Andre, I realized how exciting it was for him to come after me. He leaned in to kiss me, and I smiled. I held his dark head in my hands, pulling him to me.

He pressed me back against the couch, and I wished that I was powerful enough to cross my arms and blink twice and send us somewhere else. I wanted to take his shirt off to see the hard chest pressed against me. I wanted to watch his face when he saw me naked. Our kisses were so hard and deep, and my body was melting, wanting to join with him, wanting to be as close as possible. The club faded away around me as I held him to me as tightly as I could. Dimly I heard the first opening notes of a band warming up, but mostly all I was aware of was Andre's heart, thudding fast against mine. Blood rushed through my veins, and every cell in my body felt more alive, more sensitive, more attuned to his body than I'd ever felt with anyone before.

I pulled my head back, feeling drugged, to see his half-closed eyes glittering over me. "What?" he muttered.

"Let's go to your apartment," I said, my voice husky. I swallowed and tried to catch my breath as my words sank into his brain. He nodded and started to sit up, pulling me with him.

"Clio!"

I blinked, still dazed, and looked over to see Racey kneeling next to the couch. She had a drink in her hand and the stem of a maraschino cherry sticking out of her mouth.

"It's quarter to eleven," she said urgently, tapping her watch.

It took a moment for her meaning to penetrate my lust-crazed consciousness. "What? Not already," I said, as if denying the knowledge would make the situation go away.

She gave me a patient look, not even glancing at Andre. She'd never been like this before with any guy I'd dated. Well, okay, she'd hated Jason Fisher, but he'd been an ass.

"It's quarter to eleven," she said slowly and distinctly, trying not to say the words *you have a curfew* in front of this hot guy. A loyal friend.

What would Nan do to me if I was late? Like, if I blew off getting home anywhere close to eleven? I considered it, sitting all the way up and sipping my mojito. Ordinarily, I didn't have much of a curfew. But whenever I'd ignored her occasional request to have me home at a certain hour, she hadn't been happy. Glum memories of tons of housework made me frown.

And now, when she was already strung tight about the curse-of-the-twins thing? It would not be good.

"I have to go," I said abruptly, and swigged the rest of my drink.

"No," Andre said coaxingly. His warm hand stroked my bare arm, leaving excited little ripples in its wake. "Stay. I'll drive you home later."

"I'm going to get Della and Eugenie," Racey said, standing up. "I'll be back in a moment." *To get you* was left unsaid.

I traced the vee of warm tan skin at the collar of his shirt. "I really have to go. My grandmother needs me home early tonight. I promised her."

"Call her," Andre said, his fingers moving on me persuasively, sending shivers down my spine. "Explain. Tell her I'll see you home safely soon. Just not now."

I sighed, and Racey returned to stand by me, all but tapping her foot.

"Are they ready?" I asked, stalling.

"They're catching a ride with Susan Saltbier," Racey said. That *she* was willing to leave early with me because she had driven was not lost on me.

I thought it all through as Andre's hand curled

around my waist between the bottom of my camisole and the top of my short camouflage cargo skirt.

"Maybe Andre could drive me home," I said slowly as Bad Clio on my shoulder nodded eagerly.

"Maybe your grandmother could put your *head* on a *stake* in the front yard," Racey said, crossing her arms over her chest.

I bit my lip. She was right, of course. I would be *lucky* to get the stake treatment. *Do it now, before you weaken*, I told myself firmly while Good Clio sighed with relief. Using every bit of my willpower, I left Andre's heat and the promise of intense pleasure and stood up.

"Really?" Andre said, and my knees threatened to buckle.

I nodded mutely. Leaving now went against every desire I had. Racey pulled her car keys out of her purse and let them jingle.

Andre stood, and I loved how tall he was, at least six inches taller than me. "I'll walk you to your car," he said, running his hand through his hair and looking bummed but gallant.

"Oh, that's okay—" Racey began, but Andre cut her off.

"No. You were almost mugged earlier. I'll walk you to your car." He and Racey locked eyes for a moment, then Racey nodded and turned on her heel.

I smiled at Andre and put my arm around him as we moved through the noise of the bar.

"My hero," I said, and went on tiptoe to kiss him. He smiled and kissed me back, and I savored every second we had before we reached Racey's mom's car.

"Call me," he said as I got into the car. I nodded and kissed the hand that was leaning against the car door.

He smiled and made a tiny kissing motion with his lips, then turned and headed down the street, alone into the night.

I sighed. "You were right, Racey. You're my salvation. I thank you and I grovel before your superior sense of duty."

"Damn right," Racey said, and started her car.

A Messy Business

"Did you really think you could get away with it?" Daedalus's voice was cutting.

"Oh, Daedalus," Petra said. "Get over yourself." She ignored his look of outrage and went to the small bar. She found a bottle of spring water, then went to look out the tall French window at the people passing on the street below.

The air was heavy today, heavy and wet. She'd left Clio at home, working on her "principles of metal in magick" lesson. Clio had been only ten minutes late last night, but she was keeping a secret. Petra was sure of it. But Racey had dropped her off—so they had probably stayed together during the evening. Petra tried to control her tension. She had spoiled Clio, and now she was reaping the results. Petra was sick of secrets. Almost her entire life had been a series of secrets. After all this time, she had no idea how to live without them.

"Petra!"

Petra looked up to see Ouida coming toward her, hands outstretched. The younger woman looked a bit drawn, Petra thought. A bit tense. Well, this was a messy business.

They hugged, and Petra wondered how long it had been since they'd seen each other. Not that long, surely. Petra pulled back to look at her, smoothing her hand over the soft coffee-colored cheek. "Last time I saw you, you had cornrows and beads," Petra said, smiling.

Ouida patted her short-cropped afro. "This is easier. Wait till you see Richard."

Petra's glance was sharp. "How is he?"

Ouida nodded thoughtfully. "He's good," she said, but Petra felt her uncertainty.

The doorbell below rang, and Jules buzzed someone in. Moments later, Sophie and Manon came through the door, Sophie as lovely as always, with her fair skin and large brown eyes. And Manon still had her girlish prettiness, her pale blond curls, her dark eyes, the slender body poised on the edge of puberty.

"My dears." Petra hugged them each in turn. "Still in school?" she teased Sophie. Sophie blushed and nodded.

"Art history this time," said Manon. "But we're going to the Riviera for *Soliver*—she's promised."

"You look beautiful, my dear," Petra told Manon tenderly. Manon and Richard would always have the hardest time, and Petra understood how intensely they wished it were different.

Manon smiled and shrugged. She moved to the small sofa and sat down, propping delicate feet on the Directoire table in front of her. Petra saw Daedalus wince.

"Well, isn't this quite the little reunion?" Richard's

dry voice cut through the air. Petra turned to see him. Ouida said cheerfully, "He's goth now."

Petra embraced Richard, holding his tight body, feeling his tension. He held himself stiffly for a moment, then seemed to relax against his will, putting his arms around her in a brief, hard hug. When she looked into his brown eyes, she saw pain, as usual.

"You kept it from us," he said under his breath so only she could hear.

She nodded sadly. "I had to, love. I—"

"Yeah." Richard released himself and went to pour himself several fingers of whiskey over ice. So he was drinking again. Petra wondered how long that had been going on.

Petra looked around the room. "Where's Claire? Marcel?" Who else was missing? "And our favorite rake?" she asked dryly.

Axelle grinned, running her finger around the top of her wineglass. "He's out," she said. "Raking through the locals, no doubt."

"We can start without him," said Daedalus. "He knows all this anyway. And Claire and Marcel are on their way. Petra—we know about the twins, obviously. We know that you kept it from all of us for seventeen years. What do you have to say for yourself?"

It was a measure of Daedalus's arrogance that he was most offended by her not telling *him*—Petra was sure that if he alone had known, he would have been content to keep the secret from the others if it suited his purpose.

"I did as I thought best," Petra said calmly. "I honored Clémence's last wish, I honored the wishes of the twins' father. And truly, all this never occurred to me—" She waved her hand, summing up Daedalus's whole scheme. "Cerise's descendants have always been my responsibility—none of you have offered to take on the burden. Why would I trouble you with these orphans when you couldn't be bothered before?" She shrugged, sounding eminently reasonable.

"But surely you must have recognized the significance of twins!" Daedalus said coldly. "How many years ago did we start thinking about the possibility of a ritual? A ritual that all of us have wanted at one time or another."

"Not all of us, Daedalus," said Petra. "And frankly, after I had watched Clémence bleed to death, as I had watched Cerise's other descendants bleed to death—instantly plugging her children into your grand plan never occurred to me." Petra let her voice take on an edge of steel. Daedalus was trying to extend his influence—she would draw the line where it would stop. "I found myself with two newborn, motherless infants. Their father had no idea of Clémence's background or who I was. He was heartbroken at her death, barely able to function. He felt he could deal with only one child, if that, and begged me to take care of the other. We kept in touch for years, but gradually our letters became less and less frequent, and then he moved and left no forwarding address. I've had no idea of Thaïs's whereabouts for years."

Petra was aware that the others were watching this exchange, back and forth like a tennis match. Some would agree with Daedalus, some with her, but above all else, each witch there was truly loyal only to him- or herself.

"All that is in the past, and the twins weren't significant much before this, anyway," Ouida said. "The question is, what's happening now?"

Daedalus moved to stand before the marble fireplace, striking a pose that Petra saw as rehearsed and theatrical. Really, did he think anyone would buy this persona? Didn't he realize that the years had stripped away all their innocence forever? None of them would ever regain a fresh perspective, ever trust anything at face value, ever truly let down their guard again. Not even Sophie or Jules, who had always been the most trusting of them all.

"What's happening now is that we're working hard to put the rite together," Daedalus said pompously. "Jules, Richard, and I. And now that you're all here, we can move more quickly, with your help."

Petra put disbelief and just a touch of scorn into her voice. "The rite? *Déesse*, Daedalus, is that still the focus of your being? Have you not branched out by now?"

Daedalus schooled his face into calm, but Petra had seen the brief flash of rage in his eyes. She wondered if anyone else had. "Of course, Petra," he said. "You're not the only one who has pursued interests and achieved goals in this life. But yes, beneath all my business dealings, the companies I've founded, my pursuit of all of life's experiences, there has always been a strong interest in . . . recapturing the past, shall we say. Some of you may have let that desire go. Some of you may not agree with how urgently I feel it's necessary. But in my view, yes, the rite is imperative. I have never released that hope, never lost sight of that goal."

He managed to make everyone else sound faithless and shortsighted, Petra acknowledged wryly. Point to him.

"To what end, Daedalus?" she asked, one eyebrow raised.

"To whatever end we agree on," he came back. "That's the beauty. With this one rite, we could each achieve whatever personal goals we have. But more important, we could reclaim a treasure that was lost to us long ago, one invaluable to our ancestors. It has kept this *famille* alive. This treasure would give us, the Treize, incalculable power—and it's rightly ours. Surely you're not truly prepared to let it go forever? Does it mean so little to you, Petra? After everything?"

Petra glanced around the room—his words had made people thoughtful, perhaps given new life to dreams that she thought had been left behind long ago.

"This is all within reach again," he went on. "Now that we know Cerise's line has produced twins. They will make twelve and thirteen: a complete Treize. Not that they are the only consideration." He gestured to Jules and Richard. "Jules and I have been trying to pinpoint the exact location of the source. The land itself has shifted. Richard is working on the rite. Perhaps Sophie or Manon could help him with that. Axelle has the four cups." Axelle nodded. "Ouida has the vial of water." Daedalus deliberately met Petra's eyes. "And you have the twins. It's all coming together."

"So I assume the twins are safe, then?" Petra said sternly. "No harm will come to them from any of you?"

"Of course not," Ouida said, shocked, but Ouida hadn't been the one Petra was talking to.

"The girls are quite safe," Daedalus said with a frown. "We do, after all, need them."

Petra nodded, not meeting anyone's eyes. Inside her a feeling was rising that she recognized as panic. Ruthlessly she shut it down. Not time yet to panic, she told herself. After all, Claire was so unreliable, and she never could stand Daedalus. And then Marcel—Marcel would be a tough nut to crack. No. There was no reason to panic. Not yet. And before the time to panic came, she would have come up with a plan to save the twins, to keep them from being used in this way, in a rite that would surely kill one of them.

Thais

"I was afraid you wouldn't come back," Luc said, not looking at me.

We were headed to the levee of the river—broad steps led to a sort of boardwalk. When I'd gone to the garden earlier, he'd been waiting for me, leaning back against the vine-covered wall, his eyes closed. When I'd gotten close to him, his breathing had looked so deep and regular that I'd wondered if he was asleep. But then his eyes had slowly opened, had met mine. He hadn't smiled, but I'd felt an alertness come over his body as I approached.

I'd sat down next to him, not touching him, not saying anything.

At last he'd stood, held out one hand, and said, "Come."

I'd had no idea where he was leading me, and I didn't care. Now we were getting close to the river. I could smell the water and hear the tugboats moving barges downstream.

We walked up the steps and all the way down the boardwalk, avoiding tourists taking pictures of each other in front of the mighty Mississippi. Luc led me to where the levee was just shorn grass and crushed oyster shells. Still we walked on, until we were far away from anyone else. The French Quarter was at our backs, the river spread before us, almost a mile across. We sat cross-legged on the grass, not touching, not talking, and watched the afternoon pass by.

It was dusk before he spoke. "I was afraid you wouldn't come back." He pulled a long piece of grass out of the ground and started stripping it methodically.

"You knew I'd come back."

He turned to me then, his eyes the exact color of the darkening sky. Reaching out, he took my hand, twining our fingers together. "You're the most restful person I've ever known," he said quietly. "You have a . . . serenity, an ability to just be, without wanting anything, without needing anything. It's . . . remarkable. I actually feel almost peaceful when I'm with you." He gave a short laugh. "If you knew me better, you'd understand how amazing that is."

I felt the same way about him. "Luc," I said. A question had been on my mind since the evening he'd kissed me in the garden, stunning me to the bottom of my soul. Nothing that had happened since then detracted from how deeply he'd touched me. "What is it that *you* want from me, and what is it that you're offering me?"

His eyes seemed to grow darker, or maybe it just looked that way. A thick cloud cover had been moving over us, like God pulling a bedspread into place.

"I'm not mocking you," I said. "I really want to know."

"I know." His fingers stroked my hand while he thought. "If you'd asked me that several days ago, I would have had one answer. Now, I don't know."

I smiled, curious. "What would you have answered?"

He gave me a mischievous look that was devastating on his handsome face. "I would have said I wanted to get into your pants, and I was offering you a chance to get into mine."

I snatched my hand back. "Luc!"

He laughed, and I wanted to kiss him, hard. I blinked with surprise at that thought—not my usual kind of thing. But I felt fierce about him, as if I wanted to mark him as mine. I blushed, and Luc misunderstood.

"Have I shocked you?" he teased. "Surely you've lost count of how many guys have said that to you?"

I answered him seriously. "No, not really. I mean, people always knew that I'd say no, so they kind of quit asking."

He went still, his eyes searching my face. I realized what information I had just given up, and I groaned to myself, mortified. *Oh God, Thais, just tell him every embarrassing thing you can think of.*

"Thais." He sounded deeply shocked, and there was something else in his voice that I couldn't identify. I was smothering with embarrassment. I wanted to self-combust right there, just burst into flames and disappear into a puff of smoke.

I covered my face with my hands.

"You can't be saying—"

"I don't want to talk about it!" Without looking, I kicked him. My flip-flops had fallen off, and now he grabbed my bare foot and held it.

"Thais," Luc said, a velvet determination in his voice. He waited: as patient as time, he would sit there until I answered him.

"Thais. You're saying you've never said yes? To anyone?" He leaned closer, his voice as soothing as honey, his breath barely brushing my skin.

I gritted my teeth, pressing my covered face against my drawn-up knees, trying to make myself as small as possible—so small that I might disappear. *Good luck.*

Luc put one hand against my shoulder and one against my knee and pushed, as if I were a bear trap he was unspringing. He was much stronger than I was, and, not for the first time, I regretted not having abs of steel.

Then I was on my back on the grass, and an oddly cool, rain-scented breeze blew against my heated skin. Luc pinned my legs down with one of his so I couldn't curl up again, and I could feel him pressed against my whole length.

"Why do you want to know?" I choked out, pointlessly stalling for time—there was no way to recover from this.

"Oh, I'm very interested, Thais," he said against my ear. "I'm very, very interested."

I wanted to die. I wanted him to kiss me. I wanted ...

Again Luc waited—he had all night, wasn't going

anywhere. I had no idea what time it was or when Axelle would be back—she'd left shortly after lunch and hadn't exactly clued me in to her plans. I felt a raindrop hit my forehead. Time was running out.

"Well, if you must know," I said in a muffled, ill-tempered voice. "Then no, I haven't said yes. There, are you happy?"

I could feel him smile. He pressed his lips against my hands where they covered my face, kissing each finger.

"Not yet," he said teasingly, and I groaned and took my hands away to glare at him.

But his face, when he looked down at me, turned serious. "Why are you ashamed? It's a beautiful thing to save yourself. To not squander your beauty, your gifts, on pimple-faced, stupid boys who won't value you."

He sounded positively medieval, and I looked at him, puzzled.

"I didn't mean to embarrass you," he said, smoothing my hair away. The one drop I'd felt had presaged a fine, warm rain as gentle as a breeze—hardly more than a mist. It formed tiny, tiny diamonds on Luc's hair and gave his skin a beautiful sheen in the darkness. "I'm just surprised. It's hard to believe that someone as beautiful as you has escaped the pressure of giving yourself away."

"I got pressured," I said wryly, remembering a night when Chad's predecessor, Travis Gammel, had actually kicked me out of his car and made me walk home at *night* because I wouldn't have sex with him. Bastard. I was still mad about it.

"What stopped you?" Luc asked softly. "And don't tell me you never wanted to. I can feel passion flowing under your skin. You're made of desire."

Luc had a way of saying flowery things that sounded completely natural and sincere, even though out of anyone else's mouth they would have sounded stupid or artificial. And he was right. I had wanted to. Sometimes so much that I had felt almost crazy. But never enough to actually go ahead and do it. Now I shrugged. "Never met the right guy," I said.

One dark eyebrow rose, giving me a perfect opportunity to say, "Until you." But I didn't—couldn't. After a moment, Luc leaned over and brushed light kisses along my jawbone, making my eyes drift shut and my bones go limp.

"I guess you've said yes to millions of girls," I said, and then swallowed as an unexpected shaft of poisonous jealousy pierced me so sharply I almost gasped. The thought of him with anyone else made me feel like crying. For a long moment he looked into my eyes, and then he sat up, leaving me cold.

I realized our clothes were soaking wet from the light rain and felt many tiny drops come together to roll as one down my neck. Luc's shirt was translucent, sticking to his skin. I felt humiliated, gauche, like some stupid high-school girl. Which I was, of course.

He turned back to me, a look of gentle regret on his face.

"Not millions," he said, sounding almost sad. "But—

a lot. And until now, I never wished it were different. But you, Thais—" He leaned back down on one elbow next to me. "For the first time, I wish that I could have no memory of anyone but you."

I burst into tears, in that suave, woman-of-the-world way I have. In that moment I knew I loved him, and even more frightening, I felt he loved me. Then he was kissing me, kissing the tears in my eyes, my rain-washed face, my mouth. I smoothed my hands over his wet shirt, feeling the heat of his skin through the cloth. Our legs were tangled together, and for the first time in my life, no alarms went off in my head, no warnings told me to get myself out of there. In my mind, there was a peaceful silence, an acceptance. The warm, gentle rain drifted down on us, making me feel invisible, private, elemental.

A line from an old song floated into my consciousness, and if I had been a real witch, I would have let it float over to Luc, all raw emotion and timeless melody. It went: *I'm all for you, body and soul.*

I yawned and stretched, smiling as I relived some of last night's dreams. I had dreamed about Andre, how he looked as he came down to kiss me. I could practically feel him in my arms, feel his weight and his strength. He was perfection. It had killed me to have to leave him Friday night. Maybe today I could get away, and we could take up where we'd left off.

But first, breakfast. I could smell coffee—excellent. I rolled out of bed and headed out onto the landing. Nan's bedroom was separated from mine by a short hall that led to the one upstairs bathroom. Our house is called a camelback shotgun: you could stand in the front door and shoot a gun, and the bullet could go out the back door without hitting anything in the four rooms in between. And it was a camelback because we had only two rooms upstairs to the four rooms below. The only-two-bedrooms factor was one of the main reasons I hated the idea of Thais coming to live here.

I had others.

Glancing into Nan's bedroom, I saw her standing at

the foot of her bed. She was completely dressed, which was unusual: Sunday was our traditional laze-around, get-a-slow-start day. I wandered in, then stopped in surprise.

Nan was packing a suitcase that lay open on her bed. Q-Tip was trying to climb into it—prime napping territory—and Nan lifted him out.

"Good morning, dear," she said briskly, barely glancing at me.

"What are you doing?"

"Packing. There's coffee made downstairs, but you're on your own for breakfast."

"Why are you packing? Are we going somewhere?" A nervous flutter started in the pit of my stomach. Nan had been acting oddly since right before we'd found out about Thais.

"Not you—just me," she said, folding an Indian cotton top. She lifted Q-Tip out of the suitcase again and packed it.

"What's going *on?*"

Nan's calm, blue-gray eyes regarded me. "I need to go away for a while. I'm not sure how long. While I'm gone, you need to be extra careful, completely on guard. Don't trust anything or anyone. If anyone gives you a message they say came from me, don't believe them. If I need to contact you, I'll do it directly."

My mouth dropped open. "Where are you going? What's happening?"

"I need to take care of some things," she said. I saw

that she had gathered some spellcraft supplies—crystals, small candles, essential oils, her copper bracelets. These she now put into a purple velvet bag and pulled the drawstring.

"Tomorrow is Monday," she said. "I expect you to go to school this week, complete the metal-study course we began, and go to your tutoring session with Melysa Hawkcraft on Tuesday."

"You won't be back by Tuesday?"

"I'm not sure," she said. "I hope so, but I'm not sure. However, if I'm not back by Wednesday, I've left a letter for you in the cupboard in the workroom." She gave me a wry, knowing smile. "Don't bother trying to open it before Wednesday. It's spelled—you won't be able to. But come Wednesday, if I'm not back, you'll read it and follow the instructions inside. Understand?"

"Yeah, I guess," I said uncertainly. I hadn't told Nan about getting a knife pulled on me the other night—I didn't want her to say I couldn't go out at night with my friends or something. But now the fear of that night rushed back with all Nan's cryptic warnings and instructions. I didn't want her to go like this.

Except. I would have the house to myself.

Andre could come over. Scared was one thing I wouldn't be feeling if he were here.

Nan came over and put her hands on my shoulders. Looking deeply into my eyes, she said, "You'll be okay,

Clio. You're seventeen, and the house is spelled with layers of protection. Just watch yourself, refresh the spells every night before you go to bed, and everything will be fine." She put her head to one side, considering. "Do you want me to ask Racey's parents if you can stay over there for a few days?"

"Let me try staying on my own," I said. "If I get too freaked out, I'll go to Racey's."

"Okay." Nan hefted Q-Tip out one last time and closed her suitcase. I followed her downstairs, still in my nightgown, feeling a rising excitement. I would have the whole house to myself! The situation was clouded by worry about what Nan was going to "take care of," but still.

At the front door, Nan put down her suitcase and we hugged. I had a sudden, unreasonable fear that this would be the last time I saw her or hugged her; that from this moment on I was on my own. Sappy tears sprang to my eyes, and I blinked them back. Everything was fine—Nan said so. I would be fine, she would come back. I would have a fun little free holiday, and then she would return and our lives would go on as they had before.

I was sure of it.

"Well, *that's* bizarre," Racey said, frowning. She'd met me at Botanika after lunch. The morning, after Nan had left, had stretched out surprisingly long and quiet. I'd called Racey and left a message for Andre. He never answered his phone, it seemed. "And she didn't tell you where she was going or for what?"

"Nope. She was going out of town, not just off to a job or something." In Nan's work as a midwife, she had been gone overnight before, but just in the city. "It was weird, a bit alarming, yet—not without possibilities." I gave Racey a meaningful look.

Her eyebrows rose. "Like what?" she asked, her tone hopeful.

"A *party*, for starters," I said. "*Muchas* fiestas. All manner of merriment." I waved my hand expansively. "Blender drinks. Fun magick, depending on who we invite. Unbridled teenage mayhem."

Racey's face lit as various possibilities bloomed in her mind. "Sweet! How many people do you want to invite?"

"Enough to make it fun. Not so many that the neighbors will call the cops."

"Okay. Let's make a list," said Racey, pulling a pen out of her purse. I grinned. Racey was always very big on lists.

"The usual suspects, I assume," she said, busily writing. "And guys. I'll ask Della and Kris and Eugenie for ideas."

"Good. And let's make margaritas," I said. "And oh! Get this! I'll do a dampening spell around the house so people outside can't hear the noise from inside! Then we can have loud music!"

"Brilliant," Racey said admiringly, writing it down. "And food?"

Just then my macramé purse started wriggling on the table. Racey glanced up. "Your purse is ringing," she said briefly while I dug for my phone.

Its small screen said *unlisted number*. I clicked the answer button.

"Hello?"

"Hey, babe." Andre's voice made my skin tingle. "I got your message. What's up? Do you think you can see me today?"

"Oh, *yeah*," I said with feeling. Smiling hugely, I leaned back in my chair and tried to ignore how Racey's face had assumed a look of careful neutrality. "I can see a *lot* of you. In fact, I'm giving a party tonight—just you, me, and forty of my closest friends. Can you come?"

"At your house?" Andre sounded surprised—I'd never invited him over before.

"Yep." I gave him the address and directions on how to get there. Uptown isn't built on a grid—the streets follow the curve of the river. "Like, at nine? And—maybe you can stay and help after everyone else has gone." I was practically quivering with anticipation.

"Help with what?" Andre sounded wary.

I shrugged. "Anything that needs doing. After all, with my grandmother out of town, I'll be on my own. I'll need all the help I can get."

I could almost feel his interest quickening over the phone. "Your grandmother's out of town?" he asked. "Since when?"

"Since this morning. I didn't even know about it till I saw her packing. She'll be gone a couple days at least." For right now, I put away all my unease about when she was coming back. I would deal with it when the time came.

Andre was silent for a minute. "So you're saying that your grandmother is out of town, leaving you alone in the house."

"Uh-huh." I took a sip of my drink, careful not to make slurping noises into the phone.

"And you, being the good granddaughter who gets home on time because you promised, are immediately seizing this opportunity to raise hell."

I considered. "Pretty much, yeah."

"And, tell me if I'm getting your meaning correctly, little Clio," said Andre's dark, delicious voice, "but are you suggesting that I stay with you after everyone has left, to, um, help you with . . . something?"

I could hardly breathe. The minute the front door closed after the last person, I was going to rip his clothes off. "That's right," I managed to get out.

"Well, well, well," he said, his tone making my heart beat faster. "That sounds like a very good idea. I would love to stay later and help you—with anything you want."

With great self-control I avoided whimpering. "Terrific," I said, trying to sound together. "Anytime after nine."

"Can I bring anything? Besides myself?"

"Um, let's see." I thought quickly, glancing at Racey's list. "Can you bring some tequila? For the margaritas?"

"It will be my pleasure."

My eyes shut slowly and I swallowed. "Okay," I said, barely able to speak. "See you then." I clicked off my phone and took some deep breaths, as if recovering from running.

Racey was watching me shrewdly from across the table. "Don't tell me," she said. "Let me guess. He is, by some *miracle*, going to take you up on your offer."

I regarded my best friend. "How come you don't like him?" There, it was out in the open.

Racey looked taken aback. "I never said I didn't like him. It's just . . . you're moving awful fast. You don't really know him."

"That's never stopped us before," I pointed out. Since we were fifteen, Racey and I had been wrapping the lesser sex around our pinkies. This was the first time she had encouraged me to put on the brakes. "What is it?"

Racey shifted her weight in her seat, looking uncomfortable. "I don't know," she admitted. "He's different somehow than all the others."

"*Yeah*," I said. "Absolutely."

Racey still looked hesitant. "I don't know what it is. He just makes me feel . . . cautious."

I looked at her speculatively. Did Racey have the

hots for Andre? I didn't think so. I'd be able to pick up on it if she did. Well, they just didn't click for some reason. I wasn't going to worry about it.

"Okay," I said, switching into party mode. "Show me your list. We gotta hit the store."

Thais

"**D**amn it! *Damn it!* Where the *hell* are they?" *Crash*.

As a way to wake up, this was worse than an alarm clock but better than having a bucket of cold water dumped on my head. Next to me, Minou yawned and looked offended. I blinked groggily at my clock. Ten a.m. Another restless night had led me to sleep in.

But what was Axelle doing up so suspiciously early?

"They were right *here!*" she shrieked from the living room.

I pulled on some gym shorts and cautiously made my way out to the main room. Axelle had torn the place apart—sofa cushions on the floor, a table overturned, the basket of kindling by the fireplace knocked over. Newspapers, magazines, and clothes were strewn everywhere.

In short, the place was even more of a wreck than usual, and guess who was the only person who would care enough to clean it up?

Still shouting, Axelle picked up my French-English dictionary and heaved it across the room. It smacked the opposite wall with force, which showed me that the door to the secret room was wide open, as if the search had started up there and spilled over into the secular area of the apartment.

"Hey!" I cried, hurrying over to get the book. "That's mine!"

Axelle looked up at me, wild-eyed. I'd never seen her so wiggy—usually she moved at a slinky, feline saunter, summoning energy only to decide what shoes went with which purse. But now she looked like she'd been up for hours, and even her characteristic silky, shiny black bob was totally mussed.

"What's wrong?" I asked. "What are you looking for?"

"My cups!" she shrieked, grabbing handfuls of her hair, as if to keep a tenuous grip on her sanity. "Family heirlooms!"

I looked around, trying to remember whether I'd seen anything like that. "Were they silver, or crystal, or what?"

"They were *wood!*" Axelle cried, distraught. "Carved cypress! They're invaluable! I mean, for personal reasons! This is a *disaster!*"

"Wooden cups?" I felt a sense of dread come over me. "How many?" I already knew.

"Four!" Axelle cried, looking near tears. "Four wooden cups!" Then she seemed to catch something in my voice and looked up, her black eyes locking on me like lasers. "Why? Have you seen them? Four wooden cups?"

"Uh—" I froze like a frightened rabbit.

Axelle's eyes narrowed, and then she rushed past me into my room. I saw my pillow fly out into the hall, heard her sweep all my stuff off my desk. Minou raced out of my room and disappeared. I clenched my hands at my sides, and then Axelle tore into my small bathroom.

Her howl was a mixture of relief, rage, and triumph.

Head bowed, dreading the inevitable, I shuffled toward the bathroom. Axelle was holding her carved wooden cups—the cups that had seemed so old and battered I was sure no one would miss them from the living room armoire. Her face glowed with intense emotion as she stared at the one that held cotton swabs, the one that held cotton balls. . . .

When she spoke, her voice was low and trembling. "These four cups are the most valuable things you'll ever see in your whole life. If you had ruined them—"

There was nothing I could say. I hadn't known. If they were so valuable, why weren't they upstairs in the locked room? I mean, they weren't much to look at— just four old wooden cups.

With great effort, Axelle seemed to get herself under control. "From now on, ask if you borrow anything of mine."

This was much more reasonable than she usually was, and I nodded, embarrassed. She swept out of the bathroom, having dumped the cups' contents onto the floor, and then I heard her heading upstairs.

I sank down onto the closed toilet lid, my head in

my hands. What a way to start a Sunday. I needed to get out of here. After all the emotion last night with Luc, I felt self-conscious about going to the garden to find him, like I needed to give us both a little time and space. I was also still burning to see Clio and Petra, get some more questions answered, spend time with them. I got up and headed for the phone.

Clio

"But where does the magick come from?"

I tried to summon up patience—never my strong point. When Racey and I had gotten home, there'd been a message from Thais, wanting to come over. Well, we were having a party, the more the merrier, and after all, she was my sister.

We'd gotten a pizza for dinner, and she'd started asking about magick.

To hide my resigned sigh, I got up and went to the fridge. "Want a beer?"

Thais paused in mid-bite. "But—we're only seventeen," she said, her mouth full.

I looked at her blankly. "And . . . ?"

"Oh. No thanks," she mumbled, and I could swear a faint pink tinge flushed her cheeks.

Racey and I exchanged a look over Thais's head. I sat back down and Racey and I popped the tops on our bottles. This was like a science experiment: the whole nature versus nurture thing. Thais had grown up with our dad, who, even though I so wished I could have met him, seemed to have raised her to be a straight-arrow weenie. Then there was me. Even though Nan was strict about some things, she was pretty cool about others, and I had grown up blessedly free of most hang-ups and willing to experience life to the fullest.

"But where does the magick come from?" Thais asked again.

"Everything," Racey said. Q-Tip jumped up on the table, and she gave him a piece of her pizza cheese.

"Like Nan said, there's a bit of power, or energy, or magick in everything in the natural world," I said. "In rocks, trees, water, the earth itself. The art and craft of magick is all about learning to tap into that power."

"For what?" Thais asked. "Can I have some iced tea?"

"In the fridge," I told her. "For *what*? Because you *can*. Using magick ties you into the earth, into nature more powerfully than anything else. It's incredible."

"It's also useful," Racey pointed out. "Magick can help us make decisions, figure things out. Or be used for healing, fixing things. Or people."

"Hmm." Thais poured herself some iced tea, looking thoughtful.

"Look, I'll show you," I said, taking my plate to the sink.

"I think I'll run out and get some last-minute stuff," said Racey, getting up. "And I'll swing by my house and get some more CDs."

"Good idea," I said.

Thais looked hesitant—she'd been spooked the last time, when I'd rearranged the salt, which I had thought was so funny. But magick was one of those things that was better to experience than to hear about.

"Come on," I said briskly, looking at the clock. "We have a little bit of time before we have to get ready for the party."

Our workroom was bare except for the wooden altar and bookcases. A small cupboard stood beneath the window. I took out a piece of chalk and our four pewter rite cups. They'd been made for Nan by a friend of hers and had zodiac symbols around the edges.

First I drew most of a circle on the wooden floor but left it open. Then I got the four cups ready. "These four cups will represent the four elements," I explained.

"Four cups," said Thais, in an "ohhh" kind of way.

"What?" I asked.

"Axelle has four cups too," she said briefly, and I nodded.

"Well, she's a witch. Now, this one, in the north position, is for water, or *l'eau*. In the south, this cup holds a candle." I lit it. "Which stands for fire, or *le feu*. This incense, with its trail of smoke, represents air, or as we say in French, *l'air*." I grinned and looked over at Thais. She still looked wary, as if deciding whether she should bolt now before the naughty magick got her.

I kept on. This stuff was all so familiar and basic: *Bonne Magie*'s ABCs. "And lastly, this cup holds literal dirt, to represent *la terre*, but it could also be sand, pebbles, stuff like that. Now, step into the circle."

Thais stepped in, and I drew the circle closed. Q-Tip

wandered into the room and sat right outside the circle. He never crossed a circle line.

"Okay, now it's closed, and you can't break it until we open it again. I'm going to lead you through a basic visualization exercise," I explained. Nan had first started doing this with me when I was three years old. "Don't worry, you're not going to freak out and start tripping. Here, sit down across from me."

I set a white candle between us and gave Thais a box of matches. "Conjure fire. Just strike the match like you normally would, but say"—I did a quick translation in my head rather than start trying to teach Thais Old French— "Fire, fire, hot and light, help me have the second sight." I was pleased with myself for making it rhyme.

Thais murmured the words and struck the match as if she thought it might explode. It went out before the candle caught. She did it again and lit the candle, and then I took her hands in mine.

"Now, we both just look at the candle and sort of let our minds go," I said. "And magick will show us what we need to see."

"Is this like self-hypnosis?" Thais asked.

"Well, with self-hypnosis you're putting yourself into kind of a magickal state," I said. "You're releasing outside influences and concentrating on your inner knowledge, your subconscious. It's your subconscious that's attuned to magick."

"Oh."

"Just let your boundaries dissolve," I told Thais in a

soft, slow voice. "Become one with the fire, with me, with your surroundings. Open your mind to anything and everything. Trust *la magie* to show you what you need to know. Focus on your breathing, on slowing it down, making it so shallow and smooth you can hardly feel it."

It was interesting—when you're little and learning this, you often practice in front of a mirror. I'd spent countless hours in front of a mirror with a candle, working on being able to sink quickly and easily into the trance state that makes magick possible. Looking at Thais, holding her hands, it was eerily like those days, only this time, Thais was the mirror.

I felt myself sinking and drew Thais along with me. This was working well, despite the slight distance I felt because I'd drunk half a beer. I really had to remember the negative effect alcohol had on magick. It was a bummer.

Then, with no warning, Thais and I were standing in a *cyprière*—a swamp. It happened suddenly and abruptly, which is not usually how a vision works. And this was utterly complete—there was no sign of my workroom. I started to get a bad feeling.

Thais looked at me, startled, and I tried not to let her see my concern. "This is a swamp," I whispered, figuring they didn't have too many back in Connecticut. It was dark all around us, nighttime, and I felt a heavy, oppressive weight in the air.

Thais nodded, not looking thrilled. "I've been in a swamp," she said.

Then we saw a group of witches through the trees.

Thais gripped my hand, and I realized we hadn't let go of each other.

With dismay I recognized the huge cypress tree and the dark water bubbling up between its roots from my vision with Nan. *Déesse*. No way did I want to go through this again, and no way did I want this to be Thais's first experience with visions.

I literally backed away from the tree, starting to murmur words that would take us out of here. Nothing happened. I said the words again, sure I was remembering correctly, but still nothing happened.

"Who are they? What are they doing?" Thais whispered.

I didn't know. "I'm trying to get us out of here," I said in a low voice, as if speaking loudly would draw attention to us. The witches, all wearing long robes of different colors, some with hoods, started moving *dalmonde*, clockwise, in a circle before the tree. We heard a faint humming sound, their chanting, but I couldn't make out any words.

Thais's face was white and scared.

Before, Nan had pulled me out of my bad vision. But no one was waiting for us back at the workroom.

Boom! A burst of light and a huge shock wave of sound almost lifted us off our feet. Thais and I gripped each other's arms, our hair practically on end from electricity. I saw the circle of witches glowing as the energy entered them, saw their backs arch with either ecstasy or pain, their hands outstretched.

One of the witches was laughing—I think it was a woman. We saw another witch grab her stomach and fall to the ground. Two other witches bent over her, and even through the storm, the pouring rain that drenched us, we could hear her wails.

"Get us out of here!" Thais cried.

"I'm trying!" I told her, and repeated the words that *should* pull us right back to reality.

Time seemed to speed up. We could see everything more clearly, though we weren't too close. The witch on the ground gave birth—another witch helped the baby out, and the rain started washing it clean. It was tiny and hardly moving. Then the baby's mother sank back on the black, wet ground, her face pale and bloodless, her eyes open. Even from here we could tell she had died. The rest of the coven seemed horrified and shocked, except for the witch who was still in the throes of enjoying her surge of power.

Just like in my vision, blood was seeping into the same ground as the spring burbling up through the tree roots. I had no idea what any of this meant.

"What's that?" Thais asked, trembling, and I heard a slow bell ringing, sort of a drone.

"I don't know," I said. A woman picked the baby up and held it. The baby cried with a high, thin, kitteny sound, and I heard the bell peal again. I frowned at Thais, and she shook her head—she had no idea what it was either.

"It's the doorbell!" I cried, just as the hood of the

witch fell back. A flash of lightning lit her face, the baby, the whole circle, and the ground red with blood. In the next instant, Thais and I were blinking at each other across the lit candle in the middle of the floor. Our hands were white-knuckled, numb from clutching each other so tightly.

The doorbell rang again. Feeling shaky, I blew out the candle and stood up, quickly dismantling the circle. Thais went to open the door, moving slowly.

"Yo! Party!" Racey yelled, holding bottles above her head. A crowd of people swarmed in after her, someone put a CD into the stereo, and instantly the house was filled with noise and light and people. Q-Tip raced out the front door between their legs and escaped into the night. Smart cat. I glanced at my watch—it was past nine. I was horrified, shaken, and wanted only to go sit down somewhere and process what we'd just seen. Thais looked ill and uncomfortable. But we didn't have much choice right now.

Just as Thais was closing the door, it pushed open again and more people came in. She gave them brief, uncomfortable smiles as they all began to say hi, realized it was her, and then headed on, looking for me.

"Hi! Hi!" I said, trying to sound enthusiastic, feeling like I'd rather be anywhere but here. Fortunately, Racey was in the kitchen, already making blender drinks. Collier Collier came in with a twenty-pound bag of ice on his shoulder. I saw Della head for him, and I smiled and winked at her, feeling odd and numb. With an unhappy glance at me, Thais headed for the dining room, where Eugenie and Kris were starting to rip open bags of chips.

She didn't need to say anything. We both knew what we had seen in that last second before the doorbell had pulled us home. The older witch's hood had fallen off as she held up the newborn baby. It had been Nan. And the lightning had shown us the dead mother's face: she'd had a birthmark just like ours, a red splotch on one cheekbone.

The baby had had one too.

"Fabulous idea!" Kris said, her long blond hair swinging as she whirled past me. "Where's your trash?"

"Kitchen," I said automatically, trying to put myself into the here and now. "But we better set one up in the dining room too."

I took a deep breath and ran a hand through my hair. I had no idea what I looked like but decided I could not look very festive. I ran upstairs, tore through my closet, and pulled on a bra-strap tank and a short black skirt. In the bathroom, my eyes looked huge and haunted, but I whipped through my makeup routine and two minutes later, I ran downstairs barefoot just as the doorbell rang again.

"I'll get it!" Miranda Hughes said, grabbing the door.

Andre stood in the doorway, tall, dark, and mouth-watering, and surveyed the noisy crowd inside. I smiled, full of relief and happiness that he was here: his presence would erase the trauma of the vision. He caught sight of me, and his dark blue eyes widened in appreciation. He held up a paper bag: the tequila.

"Andre!" I called, pushing through the crowd to get to him. "Everybody, this is Andre! Andre, this is everybody!"

Laughing, he swept me up into his arms, kissing me on the mouth. I sighed with pleasure and relaxed against him, so, so happy he was here, feeling safe and cared for and not alone.

"Hey, babe," he said into my ear, and a fluttery sense of delight ran down my spine.

"Hey yourself," I said as he put me on my feet again.

Still smiling, he glanced around the room, and then suddenly, his face paled and he froze.

"What is it?" I asked. I whirled to see what he was looking at. To my surprise, Thais was standing in the dining room doorway, wearing the same thunderstruck, horrified expression that Andre had.

"Luc," she breathed, looking like death.

Thais

"Luc?" Clio said to me. "No. This is Andre, my boyfriend. Andre, this is my sister, Thais."

Luc didn't say anything, just stared at me. His face looked grim and white, and tension made his body as tight as a bowstring.

I felt like I'd been kicked in the stomach, the wind knocked out of me. I tried to swallow. Luc still had his arm around Clio's waist. I'd seen him kissing her, seen him pick her up and whirl her off her feet. Luc dropped his hand and stood apart from Clio, not touching her, and I saw a look of alarm come over her face.

"Luc," I said again numbly, my voice sounding broken, brittle as glass. By now people around us had started to realize that something weird and much more interesting than the party was happening, and heads were turning.

Just last night, we'd lain in the wet grass on the levee, and he'd held me while I'd cried and told me he wished he could have no memory of making love to anyone but me. I'd even come close to giving him that memory, against every grain of logic in me. Now I'd just seen him kiss my sister, kiss her deeply on the mouth, their hands on each other as if they knew each other very, very well. God, had *they* . . . ?

At that moment, I knew I was going to be sick. I turned and raced upstairs. I found a small bathroom and slammed the door shut in back of me. I made it to the toilet just in time, just as all the pain and horror and disbelief made my stomach turn inside out.

I don't know how long I was up there, but I had washed my face and was sitting on the floor against the tub when I realized someone was knocking on the door. If it was either Clio or Luc, I would stab them through the heart.

"Go away," I croaked, fresh tears starting to my eyes. *Stop it, idiot!* I lashed out at myself.

Still, the door opened and Della, one of Clio's friends, came in. She wore a sympathetic look and held a can of Sprite. "Drink this," she said. "It'll help settle your stomach."

Given how much alcohol I suspected Clio and her friends put away, I figured she knew what she was talking about. I took it and sipped. It was deliciously cold and fresh, and it tasted incredible. "Thanks," I muttered, feeling more wretched than I had since my father had died.

Della leaned back against the tub next to me. "Well," she said brightly, "this is one party people won't forget anytime soon."

A quick, surprised laugh escaped my throat, and I

envied her so much, to be able to look at this situation in that way. "Nope," I agreed, bleak again. "What's going on downstairs?"

"World War Three," Della said matter-of-factly. "Needless to say, people are slinking out the door as fast as they can, and the ones who want to stay and see the fireworks are getting herded out by Racey and Eugenie. So it appears your guy was two-timing you both."

A fresh pain stabbed me, and I almost choked on the Sprite. "It appears that way," I managed to say.

"Clio is furious—throwing things at him and trying to kick his ass out of here, but he's out front, saying he won't leave until he talks to you."

"Why?" I was flabbergasted. "I don't want to hear anything he says."

Della shrugged. "Don't blame you. Still, he says he's not leaving till he talks to you."

My jaw set as a welcome wave of fury lit inside me. "Fine," I snapped, getting to my feet. "I'll go talk to him."

As I stomped downstairs, I refused to dwell on how utterly humiliated I felt and instead seized the anger that was consuming me inside. In the dining room, Kris and Eugenie glanced up as they snapped plastic lids onto dip bowls. They took one look at my face and quickly feigned no interest in the horrible soap opera that was playing out in front of them.

Clio was standing in her open front door, her body arched and taut as she yelled at Luc. I saw his outline in the small front yard, right before the gate. His hands were held wide, and I couldn't imagine what he could possibly be saying to defend himself.

Clio whirled when she felt my angry footsteps vibrating the floorboards. We stared at each other, taking in the other's furious expression, and for an instant, a bolt of pain shot into my heart as I pictured her and Luc together.

"Get rid of him!" Clio snarled. "Before I start whipping steak knives at him."

I nodded grimly and strode past her to the open door. Clio crossed her arms and stood behind me. I didn't know if it was to lend support or to make sure he and I didn't somehow end up together.

"What do you want?" I demanded when I was close enough. My voice was thrumming with fury—I could hardly speak. Even to myself I sounded like a cornered, spitting cat, growling deep in its throat before it struck.

"Thaïs." Luc took a deep breath and ran a hand through his hair. He was frowning, his jaw set, his eyes dark with emotion.

"Clio told you to go," I bit out. "So go." I forbade myself to look vulnerable, hurt, or heartbroken. All of which I was, of course.

Luc glanced at Clio, then stepped forward, his eyes on my face. "Thaïs," he said again in a low voice. "I never meant to hurt you or Clio. I never meant for this to happen."

"How could it *not!*" I exclaimed. "What were you *thinking,* you bastard?"

"Neither of you mentioned having a sister," he said. "I actually didn't know if you knew each other."

"So what?" I exploded. "You knew we were sisters! Not only sisters, but twins! You knew what you were doing! And you were lying through your teeth and using us. You even gave us different names! I don't even know your name! How long did you expect to get away with it?" I shook my head in disbelief. "I know the lies you were telling me," I said in a lower voice. "I don't even want to think about what you were doing with Clio."

"Maybe he was hoping for a three-way," Clio said behind me, and I winced.

"Of course I wasn't!" Luc said angrily; then he forcibly got himself under control. He looked away from me, and it made my soul hurt to see the profile I'd traced with my fingers, my lips. I felt beyond heartbroken and didn't know how I would stand the pain.

"I'm sorry, Thais," he said. "Everything happened so fast—I didn't expect us all to take everything so . . . seriously."

I stared at him.

"But we did—and I took you both very seriously, in my way," he went on, his voice dark and strained. "Thais—my name is Luc. Luc-Andre Martin. I do live where I told you. I have been in New Orleans only a few months." He lowered his voice, his dark blue eyes focused intently on mine. "Everything I told you about how I felt about you is true. Everything I said when we were together was absolutely sincere and from my heart."

"*What?*" Clio burst out, storming past me. "So you were being sincere with *her?* What was I? *Nothing?* A *diversion?* You fricking bastard!"

"No, Clio—of course I care about you. You're beautiful. Fun and exciting. You make me forget—"

"Now you can forget about both of *us!*" I cried. "Get out of here!"

Luc looked first at Clio, then at me, and raised one hand as if to ask me for something. In his eyes I saw both regret and anger, and I hardened my heart against him.

"Thais—"

If he didn't get out of here this second, I was going to turn into a shrieking, frothing, out-of-control banshee. "You're a lying, faithless bastard," I said, speaking slowly and clearly to keep myself from breaking down. "And I'll hate you for the rest of my life." I turned on my heel and went back inside the house. Clio snapped something else at him, then she came in and crashed the door shut so hard that one of its stained glass panes cracked.

She and I were both wild-eyed, breathing hard, shaking.

"I put the guard spells back on the gate," she muttered. "Took 'em off for the party."

Racey, Eugenie, Della, and Kris peeped out from the workroom. Racey took one look at us and immediately assumed a brisk, no-nonsense control.

"Into the kitchen," she said, motioning with her hand. "Come on."

I followed Clio into the kitchen and almost fell into a chair.

"I need a shot of something," Clio said faintly. "For medicinal purposes."

"No—no alcohol," said Racey firmly. "Here. Racey's private recipe. Guaranteed to help soothe frayed nerves." She poured two cups of a steaming herbal tea and set them in front of us.

Mindlessly I took my cup and drank, not caring that it was too hot. I saw Clio pass her hand over her cup, as if to feel the steam, and then she drank without wincing.

Within two minutes I felt like someone was smoothing aloe on all the burning pain inside me, over my heart that felt wrapped in barbed wire, around my mind that felt like acid had been dumped on it. The tea was putting out fire after fire, and I found I could almost think clearly.

"I feel better," I said, looking up at Racey. "Thanks. I'll have to get that recipe."

She smiled at me. "You'll be able to come up with one yourself soon."

I put my head in my hands. She meant if I learned magick. Which reminded me of the awful vision Clio and I'd had, right before Luc had ripped our hearts out.

This was pretty much one of the top-three worst nights of my entire life.

"I think we're going to go," said Della. "Unless you need us to stay."

Clio shook her head and drank more tea. "No," she

said, her voice thin. "Thanks, guys. And thanks for cleaning up and everything."

"I'll call you tomorrow," Eugenie said. Clio gave a wan smile and nodded.

"Want me to stay?" Racey asked after the other three had left.

Clio glanced up at me and bit her lip. "That's okay," she said softly. "I guess we can take it from here. But thank you." She stood up and hugged Racey.

"Yeah, thanks for the tea and being here," I added inadequately. Racey patted my shoulder, picked up her purse, and left.

And Clio and I were left alone.

If I looked as bad as Thais did, I was seriously going downhill. Her face was pinched and bloodless, and her shiny black hair lay limply on her shoulders.

"I think I'll go too," Thais said, starting to get up. "I just want to go to bed."

"How are you going to get home?"

"Streetcar," she said, putting her teacup in the sink.

"Not this late. I'll drive you home."

She looked like she wanted to refuse, but she was too sensible to. "I wish I'd never come to New Orleans!" she burst out.

That makes two of us. My skin was crawling: Andre had actually meant what he'd said to Thais, and I had been just the good-time girl. He might even love her. *Her.* He hadn't left until *she'd* come down and talked to him. Even out on the porch, it was *her* understanding he'd wanted, not mine. He'd kept talking to *her*, explaining to *her.* Oh yeah, I'd been beautiful and exciting and fun. Yay for me. But he'd *cared* about *her.* I felt like I was going to shatter into sharp, bitter shards, like colored glass.

I drank my tea, trying to think about anything else.

Unbidden, the image of the crying newborn popped into my mind. Why had we seen that? Why had it all been so real? Because we were doing it together?

"Who do you think that baby was earlier?" I asked, and Thais blinked at the shift in gears.

"Uh, I don't know," she said. "I was thinking maybe our mom? Dad told me that Mom had this same birthmark." She touched her cheekbone lightly. "He thought it was so strange that I had it too—birthmarks aren't usually inherited."

"So you think it was real, what we were seeing?"

Thais looked up, surprised. "You mean, maybe it wasn't? Do you usually see real things or just possibilities, or even stuff that never happened and couldn't happen?"

I thought. "All of the above," I decided. "But that one felt so real, more real than they usually do. Sometimes it's like watching TV, kind of, where you're still aware of your surroundings. That one was so complete. I wish Nan were here to talk about it."

"Where is she, anyway? Isn't she coming back tonight?"

Amazingly enough, it was barely ten o'clock. It felt like three in the morning.

I shook my head. "She had to go out of town for a little while. She should be back in a day or two." I hoped. Memories of how I'd planned to spend my free days—and nights—made my teeth clench.

"You're lucky," said Thais. "I wish Axelle would go

213

out of town. For a long time." Suddenly she looked over at me. "Did you love him?" she asked in a broken voice, her face miserable.

I let out a slow breath. "No," I lied. "I was just using him. He was hot, you know? And I wanted a fling. But I'm still *really* pissed," I added.

She nodded. It was so obvious that she'd really loved him too. She sighed and I could practically see her heart bleeding inside her. I wondered if we were linked somehow—I'd heard of twins who could finish each other's sentences and did the same things at the same time, even if they were in different cities. And those twins weren't even witches, like us.

"Can I go home now?" she said. "Are you sure I shouldn't take the trolley?"

"Not this late. It's not safe. Hang on and I'll get my purse. And I'm going to change." I hated this skirt, hated this top, never wanted to see them again. I headed upstairs and heard the front door open.

"I'm going to wait on the porch," Thais called. "Get some air."

"Okay," I called back. In my room I put on gym shorts and an old T-shirt and pulled my long hair back into a ponytail.

Pathetic, desperate thoughts swirled around me like dust devils. Maybe Andre was still outside. Maybe they would both be gone when I got out there. Or maybe after I dropped Thais off, I would see Andre on the street, and he would be so miserable and tell me he had been trying not to hurt Thais's feelings, but it was me he loved. . . .

I raced out through the house and found Thais by herself on the front porch, looking up at the stars.

"It was cloudy earlier," she said, sounding like she'd been crying. "Now it's clear."

"Yeah." There was a bitterness at the back of my throat that I couldn't swallow away. My blue Camry was parked on the street: hardly anyone has a garage in New Orleans, and not many people even had driveways.

Thais went out through our front gate while I locked the door behind me. I felt drained, totally spent and exhausted, and just wanted to get rid of Thais so I could go collapse in bed and cry without anyone seeing.

I started down the front steps, and just as I reached the front gate, I heard a dull buzzing, humming sound that was growing louder with every second. I looked up at the overhead telephone and electricity wires—was something going funky? Was it music from somewhere?

"Clio!"

I snapped my head down to look at Thais, then gasped. A huge dark cloud was moving toward her fast. "Thais!" I yelled. "Get back inside the gate!"

But it was too late—the dark cloud enveloped her, and she screamed. In horror I realized it was a cloud of *wasps*, a huge, droning mass of angry wasps, and they were attacking her. In the next second I realized that this was unnatural, that wasps didn't do this. Which meant they'd been sent on purpose, to harm Thais or me or both. Rushing out the gate, I started a dispelling spell, drawing the powerful protective sign of *ailche* in the air, followed by *bay*, the sign for wind.

"Clio!" Thais shrieked, the sound muffled.

"I'm coming!" I yelled, and then I dove into the middle of the cloud and grabbed her. If I could pull her back inside the gate, the protection spells should help. Suddenly it felt like a thousand hot needles plunged into my skin, and I cried out. Thais was crying, waving her arms, lurching around, and I started pulling her back toward the gate.

I was frantic: my eyes were swelling shut, one wasp stung me inside my ear—my entire being was a mass of burning pain. I shouted a banishing spell, and it seemed the droning let up for just a second, but then the wasps were around us again, so thickly that I couldn't even see the gate or the house. The two of us stumbled off the curb into the street—we'd gone in the wrong direction!

"Thais!" I shouted. "Give me your energy!"

"Wha—I can't!" she cried, sounding hysterical.

"Just send me your energy, your strength—any way you know!" I yelled. "Think!"

I had her by both shoulders. My hands were so swollen and numb that it felt like my skin was splitting. Everything in me wanted to scream my head off and run a hundred miles, but I forced myself to stand still and concentrate, trying to ignore the pain, ignore the burning, salty tears running down my swollen, stinging face.

"*Ailche*, protect us!" I said, crying, my tongue thick. "*Bay*, dispel this swarm! *Déesse, aidez-nous!*" I concentrated on Thais, pushing past her outer, terrified body and into her core, where her unawakened energy lay. It was familiar to me, similar to mine, and I sought out the power she didn't know she had. I joined my power to hers and repeated my banishing spell:

> Force of darkness, leave us be
> Your power's gone, your secret found—
> My twin has given strength to me
> Three times this curse on you rebound!

My eyes were almost completely swollen shut, but my ears heard the droning lessen, and I thought I felt fewer new stinger jabs. I risked opening my eyes and saw that the swarm had in fact started to disperse, untidy clumps of wasps staggering through the air as if unsure of how they'd gotten there or what they were doing. Our feet were covered with wasp bodies.

A minute later, they were all gone, and Thais and I were standing in the street. Amazingly, no neighbors had come out to see what the shouting was about, but they might have been spelled to stay indoors.

"Come on," I said, barely understandable. My tongue filled my mouth, and I knew we needed help fast—we'd both been stung hundreds of times.

Thais was shaking, sobbing, her eyes shut, her grossly bloated arms still covering her head. I took her shoulder and started towing her back to the house. In my mind, I sent one of my teachers, Melysa, an urgent help message. I couldn't talk on the phone at this point, and I didn't know how much time we had.

Before now, I'd always had Nan to help me if I was in trouble or hurt. I'd depended on her to fix everything. With her gone, I had to be the strong one, the one who saved us.

"I hate this place!" Thais sobbed thickly. "Sheets attack you here, trucks drive through streetcars, and now killer wasps! This place is a death trap!"

"Shh, shh," I said, gently pulling Thais through our garden gate. We stumbled up the porch steps, and I had a hell of a time stuffing my hand into my pocket to fish out the house key.

I was barely able to turn the key, and then I felt Melysa coming, running down the street. She lived only three blocks away—she was one of Nan's best friends, one of the top witches in our coven, and had been tutoring me in healing spells for the past year.

She burst through the gate, her full, wavy gray hair flying. "Clio!" she exclaimed, looking at us.

I made a mumbled "uunnhhh" sound.

"Inside, inside," Melysa said, careful not to touch us.

I was starting to feel dizzy, light-headed, and oddly cold. I couldn't think straight, couldn't explain Thais to Melysa or even tell her what had happened. My world was narrowing, growing chilly and black around the edges, and then I felt myself falling, falling in slow motion.

Thais

A heavy weight was on my chest, making it hard to breathe. Alarmed, I opened my eyes.

A broad white furry face was looking back at me. Q-Tip.

"Jeez, kitty—you've got to take dieting seriously," I murmured, easing him off my chest. Ah. I could breathe again.

So I was at Clio's. This must be Nan's room. I got out of bed and moved slowly to the door, feeling like I'd been hit all over with a baseball bat. Out on the landing I suddenly remembered the whole horrible night before. It had started with finding out that I had meant nothing to Luc and ended with wasps almost killing me. I glanced at my arms—I had faint pink spots all over me, hundreds of them, but they were hardly noticeable.

I looked into Clio's room. It was empty.

Downstairs, I padded barefoot into the kitchen. Clio sat at the small table, her hands wrapped around a mug. When she looked up at me, her green eyes were clear and weirdly calm.

"Coffee?" she asked.

"God, yes," I said, and poured myself a cup.

"Tell me again what you said last night about being attacked by sheets and streetcars and stuff," she said.

"Oh my God, Axelle!" I remembered, my hand over my mouth. She was going to be furious! I'd stayed out all night—

"Melysa called her," Clio told me. "She knows where you are. It's cool. And I called us in sick this morning to school."

School—jeez, school was the last thing on my mind. "Was Melysa the woman with gray hair?" I asked, barely able to remember what she looked like, only that she had been calm and kind and had taken all my pain away. She was no doubt a witch, I thought with resignation.

"Yeah," Clio answered. "She's one of my teachers. She's a healer, and she lives close by, so that was lucky. She left early this morning."

I sank down into a chair, shivering at the memory of the wasps. "That was very bad," I said, and Clio nodded.

"Yes. Now tell me again what you said last night. What's happened to make you think New Orleans is a death trap," Clio pressed, calm and unstoppable. She seemed unlike herself this morning, older somehow, less offhand. Well, near death can do that to a girl.

"I had a bad dream," I said, still hating to think of it. "An incredibly realistic dream where I was in a swamp. A huge snake came and wrapped itself around me, choking me. I felt like I was dying, couldn't breathe. Somehow I yelled, and then Axelle came in—though

220

my door was locked—and she woke me up. My sheet was twisted into a thick rope, and it was wrapped around my neck tight enough to choke me. I had bruises for days, as if I'd been strangled." I shivered. Clio was listening intently, following every word.

"And then on the second day of school, I was on the streetcar, going to school. A teenager driving a pickup truck jumped the curb and hit a light post. It snapped off and crashed through a closed window on the street-car—right where I'd been sitting until like a second before. If I hadn't moved, it could have killed me. And now the wasps. I mean, God."

Clio nodded, thoughtful.

"Why?" I said.

"A few nights ago, a mugger pulled a knife on me," she said. "He didn't even really try to rob us, me and Della, Eu, and Racey. What he really wanted to do was knife me. Me in particular. And then the wasps last night. And your dream and the streetcar. I mean, sud-denly it seems so clear, right? Someone's trying to kill us. Someone from Nan's old *famille* has found out about us and is trying to kill us because we're twins."

My stomach dropped. "You're right," I said, shocked. "That has to be it. But who? If Axelle wanted to kill me, she could have done it a long time ago. She's the one who saved me from my dream. Same with Jules and Daedalus—Axelle isn't always there. They could have gotten to me far more easily before now."

"And it's not Nan," Clio said wryly.

"Who else is there?" I asked, trying to think.

Clio shrugged. "It could be anyone from their *famille*. Which could be . . . let's see—there were fifteen original families three hundred years ago. Now we have all their descendents. It could be more than a thousand people."

"Great," I said, wanting to race back to Welsford on the next plane. But they'd found me there—I wouldn't be any safer now.

"Nan isn't here to ask," Clio said. "Of course, now I wish I'd told Nan about being mugged."

"Well, I can think of one place to start," I said. "Axelle."

We found Axelle standing in the kitchen, eating cold leftover Chinese food out of its carton.

"Are you all right, then?" she asked, examining me.

"Yes," I said. "But it wasn't pretty. This is Clio."

Clio looked around the apartment—it had quite a different ambience than the comfortable, homey place she shared with Nan.

Axelle studied Clio. "Interesting," she said, and I realized that Clio and Axelle were somewhat alike in their personalities. They were both kind of showy and used to getting their own ways. Axelle was just a more exaggerated version.

"We want some answers," Clio said coolly. She pulled up a chrome-and-leather bar stool and sat down. Axelle looked at us both, a little smile playing around her lips.

"I'm so happy to meet you," she said in an attractive, cultivated voice, and hugged Clio first. When she hugged me, I felt warm and happy. "I'm Ouida Jeffers, and I'm a good friend of . . . Petra's. Now let me see. . . ." She looked at us both, then nodded at Clio. "You're Clio, and you're Thais," she said to me. I nodded, smiling at her. She seemed blessedly normal and unweird. "I know this is all strange and confusing—maybe a little scary? I wish Petra was here today to help. But she'll be back soon."

"Where did she go?" Clio asked quickly.

Ouida patted her arm. "It will all be clear soon," she promised. "Today might be upsetting for you—but afterward, maybe we can all go out and get something to eat somewhere? I'm anxious to know you both better."

"I'd like that," I said, feeling more comfortable than I had in days.

The doorbell rang again, and Axelle yelled, "Come in!" The apartment had taken on a party atmosphere, with people getting themselves things to drink, milling around, talking. Yep, just a bunch of modern witches hanging out, schmoozing. . . . I wondered if Ouida would be interested in escaping sometime soon.

The door opened, and—

My heart pounded one last time and thudded to a halt. I saw Clio turn; then her body froze and the hand holding her glass clenched.

"Luc," Richard said casually, tossing a pecan into his mouth.

Daedalus and Jules nodded at him. Luc nodded back at them. Axelle waved at him as she talked to Sophie. Luc ran one hand through his dark hair and nodded back. He looked tense, upset.

Clio turned very slowly in her seat and met my eyes. I'm sure we wore the same sick, horrified expression: the situation that had already been as wretched and heart-breaking as it possibly could be had just gotten worse.

Luc was one of *them*.

Clio

Okay, call me impulsive. It took only a few seconds to process Andre's presence, meet Thais's eyes, and then take aim and hum my heavy glass hard at Andre's head. Being a *witch*, he felt it coming at the last second and managed to deflect it, just barely. It whisked by his head, splashing his shirt, and he stared at me, grimly shocked.

Instantly his eyes shifted, looking for Thais. He saw her standing behind the kitchen counter, and the new wash of pain in his eyes made my insides twist.

Of course, all conversation stopped, and the other seven witches now stared at the stupid, humiliating drama spread before them. Andre was a witch, and brilliant me had been so lust-crazed and in love that I had totally missed it. I'd been so swamped by my raging emotions that I'd thought the strong vibes I got from him were all sexual attraction.

My stomach dropped at my next thought. Could it be Andre? Could it have been Andre who was trying to kill us? He'd lied about so many other things. . . .

I sucked in a silent breath and spun on my bar stool, my back to Andre. I met Thais's eyes, letting my feelings show, and I saw the dawning comprehension in hers. A new stunned look came over her face, and then she looked at me like, *Do you really think so?* I shrugged, then stared stonily out the small kitchen window behind Thais. I didn't know anything anymore.

"Good God, Luc, already?" Axelle's tone was both amused and irritated.

"Luc, I told you this—" the old guy, Daedalus, began, but Andre cut him off.

"Shut up." He sounded furious.

Thais's eyes were downcast, looking only at Axelle's black cat as she stroked it.

Richard gave a somewhat bitter-sounding laugh. "The more things change, the more they stay the same, eh, Luc?"

"Shut up!" Andre snapped again, and Richard made a "whatever" gesture.

I felt a soft hand on my back and tensed, ready to smack whoever it was. "I'm sorry, Clio," Ouida whispered, then sighed heavily. "I should have come back weeks ago."

"It doesn't matter," I said stiffly. I turned around again and faced Axelle, who was still carrying on a silent, exasperated conversation of gestures with Andre.

"So are we all here?" I said, making my voice as cold as possible. "Why don't you get this show on the road? Is anyone going to tell us what the hell is going on?"

I heard Richard chuckle behind me and resisted the strong temptation to turn around and deck him.

"Yes," Axelle said. "I think it's time to initiate our newest members."

I frowned. Not exactly what I had in mind. "I want some answers first. Who are you?"

The older guy stepped forward. His practiced smile reminded me of a circus ringmaster. How appropriate. "We are members of the *Treize*," he said. His open hands encompassed everyone in the room. "As are you and your sister."

Huh. "Okay, *Treize* means 'thirteen' in French, so I'm guessing you're a coven. But how does my grandmother fit into all this? We already belong to a coven."

"Petra belonged to this one first," said Jules. "We don't get together very often."

"To put it mildly," said Richard, under his breath.

"How are Thais and I members of this so-called coven too?" I asked.

"This coven is made up of members from the fifteen original families who founded our ancestors' settlement hundreds of years ago," Daedalus went on. "Not every family is represented, of course. But the twelve of us, plus one of your ancestors, a woman named Cerise, made up our coven. Cerise died . . . long ago, and another member disappeared and is presumed dead. So we've been only eleven for a long time. But then one of Cerise's descendents, your mother, Clémence, had twins. So you and Thais unexpectedly make a full thirteen possible again."

Eyes narrowed, I looked around at all the witches in

the room, carefully avoiding Andre. Even seeing him hurt unbearably. There was something weird here—I mean, something even weirder than all the obvious weirdness.

Thais spoke up. "Even with us, there are still only ten people here."

"Your—Petra is out of town," said Jules. "And two other members haven't arrived yet."

"But they will," Daedalus said firmly.

"Wait a second." I held up my hand. "All of you were members of the Treize?"

Axelle nodded, shrugging, and Daedalus said, "Yes."

"And now you found out that we're twins and that we're almost ready for our rite of ascension." I was, anyway. "So we'd be useful in a coven."

"Yes, my dear," Daedalus said, practically rubbing his hands together.

"Okay. Explain *them*," I said bluntly, pointing at Richard and Manon. Who clearly weren't anywhere close to seventeen, especially Manon.

Awkward silence.

"She's smarter than the average bear," Richard said dryly, and I spun on my bar stool.

"Shut *up*, you weird kid!" I hissed, and he raised his eyebrows and looked back at Axelle.

"You're right, of course," Ouida said, glancing at the others in the room. "And being a witch yourself, you understand that there are often mysteries and things that aren't how they appear on the surface."

"Why don't we have a circle," Jules suggested. "It would be a good place to start."

Being smarter than the average bear, I knew that having a magick circle with a bunch of strangers, one of whom I thought might be trying to kill me and Thais, was not a good idea. I started to say so, and then I caught Ouida's face.

She looked accepting, as if she knew what I was thinking and it was okay. She would support whatever decision Thais and I made. Assuming we had a choice about this. I turned around, and Thais and I met eyes. Her shoulders gave a tiny shrug, as if to say, *Maybe we should.*

I nodded. Maybe one or more people here were dangerous to us. But not all of them. Not Ouida. Probably not Axelle, Daedalus, or Jules, according to Thais.

Thais came and stood next to me. Together we faced Daedalus. "Okay," I said.

Thais had told me about Axelle's secret room upstairs. We went up. It looked like any other witch's workroom. I stayed close to Ouida, hating being in the same room with Andre. Worse, I hated his being in the same room as Thais. All my senses were on alert, watching to make sure they didn't somehow end up together, and not just because I thought he might be trying to hurt us. I knew this was sick and paranoid of me, but I couldn't help it.

Daedalus drew a large circle on the floor. Axelle got four old wooden cups and set them in the points of the compass, with their respective elements. Feeling someone's eyes on me, I glanced up to find Andre watching me. As soon as I saw him, he looked away. He still seemed tight and angry, and his face was pale and unshaven, as if he hadn't slept well last night.

Good, I thought. *I hope he never sleeps well again.* I started to think about spells to accomplish this, conveniently forgetting the threefold rule, and then Axelle said, "Everyone join hands."

Ouida was on one side of me. On my other side was Sophie, who seemed nice and shy and had a stronger French accent than most of them. Next to her was Richard, then Andre, then Jules, Thais, Manon, Daedalus, and Axelle on Ouida's other side.

Daedalus started chanting, and we began to walk slowly *dalmonde*. I actually didn't recognize what Daedalus was saying—it sounded like it might be Old French, but I could make out only a few words: *vent* and *pierre, cercle, plume*. Wind and stone, circle, feather. They didn't make sense. The others joined in, but Thais and I met eyes and shrugged. My sister looked curious and cautious but kept in step and carefully walked right inside the large circle.

We began walking faster as their voices seemed to separate like ribbons to intertwine and lace through and under and around each other. This happened in my regular coven too, and I always loved this part, the weaving together of the whole. Wisps of magick started to swirl around us, like fine threads of cotton candy. I waited for the familiar rush of magick to fill me, but I felt dull around the edges, not fully present.

Against my will, I glanced across the circle and saw Andre watching Thais. She wasn't looking back. Quick rage filled my chest, and I realized that my anger was getting in my way.

It was almost impossible to release it. I wanted to rake my fingernails down his face—almost as much as I wanted to grab him and kiss him hard, make him forget my sister. Gritting my teeth, I closed my eyes and took several deep breaths, putting both of them out of my mind. I tried to release all emotion, all feelings, to open myself to receive magick.

We quickened our pace, and I kept my eyes closed, concentrating on being here and being blank, a blank canvas for magick to color. I caught more words: *calice, l'eau, cendres.* Chalice, water, ashes. No idea what they meant. But at last it worked: a familiar excitement and anticipation came over me, and magick began to swell within my chest. I breathed it in like light, letting myself feel the joy, the completeness of being sur-rounded by magick. It dwarfed everything else, and from this exalted height, my anguish over Andre's betrayal seemed far away.

I opened my eyes and looked at Thais, wondering what she was thinking and feeling. Her eyes were open wide, as if in astonishment, her face transformed from wary to welcoming. I smiled at her, and she smiled back breathlessly. She felt the exhilaration of magick too, and it was her first time. I was glad we were together now, despite all the mixed feelings I had about her, about us, about our future.

I felt the lovely rush of power and life, felt myself meld with the other forces in this circle, that heady sense of connection, the joining of spirits. Our circle moved swiftly, round like the earth, like the sun, eternal like the tides of the oceans. The chant reached a crescendo and I found myself joining in: *Un calice du vent, un cercle des cendres, une plume de Pierre, un collier d'eau.* Again and again we sang the words, and though I thought I got their translation, they still didn't make sense to me. I offered up a prayer to the *Déesse*: please help me and my sister become what we are supposed to become. Please help us keep safe.

Then, as if one, the circle suddenly stopped. We threw our hands in the air, releasing our energy, sending out our power, which is the only way to receive the power back into you. I felt stronger within myself, felt I could work miraculous spells, and then Ouida and I were smiling and hugging.

The ten of us were flushed, panting, glorying in the aftereffects of magick. Thais was hugging Sophie. Hating myself, my eyes sought Andre. His face was dark, he was breathing hard, his emotions jangled and discordant. He looked like he had when we were twined together, kissing, when I had been offering him everything, and he had almost taken it. I sent out a quick

234

general thanks that we hadn't actually gotten farther than that.

Then Thais was in front of me, blocking my view. I saw faint tear tracks on her pink cheeks as she put her arms around me. I hugged her back, feeling less alone, less wretched. I had a sister. I think it truly only hit me right then: I had a *sister*, forever. We shared the same blood, the same bone. We were one person, split into two. We would never be alone again. It seemed huge and amazing in a way that it hadn't until then, and my eyes filled with tears.

"What did you think?" I whispered.

Her face, so eerily like my own, was solemn. "It was . . . scary," she said finally, trying to gather her thoughts. "And . . . so beautiful. I wish—" She broke off, biting her lip. "I wish I had never known of anything so beautiful, so powerful." Her face was almost sad.

"What do you mean? I don't understand."

"Before, I didn't know what I was missing," she said softly. "Now I do. And now I know . . . I have to have it. I'll do anything to feel it again."

I nodded. What has a front has a back. And the bigger the front, the bigger the back. The joy and beauty of magick were married to the awful responsibility of wielding it. The pleasure of calling on magick was tempered by the need to do so.

"Did you get any of the words?" she asked me.

I nodded. "Some, but they didn't make sense. Part of it was, 'A chalice of wind, a circle of ashes, a feather of stone, a necklace of water.' All connected like that."

Thais looked thoughtful, repeating the words to herself. "You don't know what it meant?"

"No—never heard it before. We can ask Ouida," I said.

"Now I think it's time." Ouida's clear voice cut through the lingering effects of the magick. "Time to know the truth. The whole truth."

Thais

Maybe I'd had enough truth for one day. I felt drained. My skin was still alive and glowing from what I'd just discovered. I didn't know how it had happened, where it had come from, or even what "magick" really was. I only knew that I'd felt it, and for a few minutes, I'd been part of everything. I hadn't been alone, everything had made sense, and my pain had lessened. If that was magick, sign me up.

"Can we go back downstairs?" Manon asked in her little-girl voice. "It's hot up here."

The whole truth. I thought about finding Clio, realizing she and Petra were witches, finding out Luc was really Andre, finding out he was a witch. I really didn't think I could take any more. Could I escape somehow? But Ouida seemed to have a plan, and Clio looked determined.

Downstairs, every time I glanced at Clio, she was watching Luc. Her face was angry, but I recognized another emotion as well: desire. She'd said that she'd just been using him, that she didn't love him. It wasn't true. She'd wondered if he was the one behind the attacks. I didn't know—when I tried to follow that line of thought, my brain just shut down.

"Sit here, Thais," said Ouida, gesturing to the sofa. I was stuck. Clio sat at the other end of the sofa, and Richard sat between us. I couldn't wait to hear *his* story.

Axelle, Ouida, Daedalus, and Jules all looked at each other, as if silently figuring out who should start. My curiosity was mixed with dread about what might be coming. After today, everything that had happened in my life before New Orleans would be gone forever, as if it had happened to someone else. I felt Luc's eyes on me and Clio's eyes on him. I ignored him as best I could, but heat rose in my cheeks just from being in the same room.

"Well, really, our story started quite a long time ago," Ouida said slowly. "Our families came from France, through Canada, and settled in southern Louisiana, not far from New Orleans. That was in the late 1600s. There were fifteen families, fifty-eight people total. They lived in peace and made their lives and homes in their new chosen land. They practiced *Bonne Magie* and stayed true to the old ways.

"This continued for almost a hundred years," Ouida went on. "As with any group of people, there were leaders and followers—people who were stronger and people who were weaker. Within the fifteen families and the new families that had been created by intermarrying, there were several different covens."

"Eight, I think," said Jules, frowning in thought.

"Now, I have to tell you a bit about *Magie Noir*," Ouida said, taking a deep breath.

"Dark magick?" Clio said in surprise.

"Yes," Ouida went on more firmly. "In our community, young people, teenagers, often experimented with *Magie Noir* before they made their rite of ascension. The corollary today would be experimenting with drugs, or drinking, or sex."

"Or all three," Richard murmured, and my skin crawled. Bizarrely, there was something very likable about Richard, but he was also just so young to be so dark. It was creepy.

"In those days, it was usually *Magie Noir*," Ouida said. "They were punished if caught, but in general the feeling was that they would play with it, get it out of their systems, and then be ready to settle down into the community as they should. And for the most part, that's what happened."

"Until Melita," Daedalus said, his voice heavy with memory, as if it had all happened just last year.

"Yes," Ouida said. "Until Melita. Melita was a very powerful witch, with the kind of power that comes along once every hundred years. She learned fast, soaking up information, rites, history like a sponge. Before she was sixteen, she made her rite of ascension, thus giving her even more power."

I had been watching Ouida, but when I looked around the room, I was surprised by people's expressions. Almost everyone here wore a mantle of gloom. These witches who only ten minutes before had been singing with clear joy now looked like they were immersed in sadness and pain. I risked glancing at Luc, and he looked even worse than before. He met my eyes, a still, speculative look on his face. I shifted and looked away from him, my heart pounding.

"The community ignored what was happening and closed their eyes to the fact that Melita wasn't just passing through her *Magie Noir* phase—she was reveling in it, pursuing it, and working hard to increase her power all the time, through dark and dangerous methods."

Jules lowered his head and rubbed his eyes with one hand, as if suddenly tired beyond words. Daedalus for once had no used-car-salesman's smile, but looked drawn and stiff.

"One night Melita was in the woods, performing her dark rites. It's still unclear whether she caused this to happen or whether it was just there and she found it—but she came upon a small, bubbling spring, *un Source*. The water was red-tinted and very cold, and she drank from it."

"She said she made it, conjured it," said Richard, and Daedalus whirled on him.

"I don't believe it. It was sheer happenstance that led her to it."

"However it happened," Ouida continued, "from that day on, Melita was never ill. When the whole community had the flu and more than twenty people died, Melita never got sick. Any small injury healed unnaturally quickly. She was strong and healthy in a way that few people were in those days, before antibiotics and vaccinations. But more important, her magick increased maybe a hundredfold.

"Several years passed. There had always been people whose magick seemed stronger or more true, but now Melita overshadowed the best of them. It was obvious that she had special powers. The boys in the village fell in love with her, but she didn't care for them—only for power. She began to dominate the whole community, both through her force of will and by her magick. The *Magie Noir* had taken hold of her, and unlike other people, it didn't let her go."

"She studied the ancient texts," Jules said quietly. "And researched herbology and astrology. Within seven years, she was the strongest witch anyone had ever seen. At the end of this seven years, Melita had devised a plan to forever consolidate her power by a ritual at the Source, this time with twelve carefully chosen fellow witches. These witches would represent a cross section of abilities, affinities, ages, sexes, and so on, as her research had indicated was necessary."

"There was an older man," said Daedalus, his voice dull. He was looking at the floor and didn't raise his eyes. "An elder in the community—the mayor, if you will."

"There was a powerful, headstrong woman," said Axelle, sounding sad and un-Axelle-like.

"There was a virginal young woman," said Sophie, not looking at anyone.

"There was an older woman, a wise healer," Ouida said. "And there was a female slave."

"And another slave," said Jules. "Arrogant and ambitious."

"There was a girl," Manon said slowly. "Who had not yet reached puberty."

"There was a heartless rake," said Luc wearily.

It was then that all the hairs on the back of my neck stood up, and my blood turned cold. My breaths became faster and shallower, and I watched this play unfold with horror.

"There was a boy." Richard's voice was bitter and full of pain. "Halfway to becoming a man."

"There was an innocent young man," said Ouida, "who was emotional and easily led."

"There was the village outcast, a woman of loose morals," said Daedalus with distaste.

"And there was Melita's younger sister, Cerise," said Axelle. "She was unmarried but pregnant. No one knew who the father was."

"The baby was due in two months," said Sophie, sounding near tears.

My eyes wide, I sought out Clio's face. Silent knowledge passed between us: our vision. They were describing our vision. Holy crap.

"Through various means—bribes, threats, coercion—she rounded up these twelve witches and performed the ritual with them," Ouida said. "During the ritual, they all drank from the spring, thereby increasing all their magickal powers—beyond where Melita's had been."

"During the rite, Melita called on all the dark forces she knew," Sophie said softly. "Forces the others didn't know existed. And her magick was so strong, and the combined forces of the thirteen were so strong, that it called down the wrath of heaven."

My eyebrows must have gone up because Ouida explained, "It called down a tremendous surge of power that entered Melita and poured into the souls of the twelve with her."

"Dark power," Jules said.

"It stunned everyone," said Manon, her voice wispy and light. "It felt . . . like the beginning and the end of everything, of life itself."

"Which it was, in a way." Luc sounded very tired.

"No one knows why, but Cerise went into early labor," Ouida continued. "The rest of the twelve were practically glowing in the dark with power and magick and energy, but it didn't have the same effect on Cerise. She went into labor and died in childbirth."

I almost said, "But the child lived," thinking of the pale, mewling baby washed clean by the rain.

"Maybe Melita knew it would happen," Richard said. "Maybe not. But Cerise, her sister, died that night."

"The eleven others who were left were horrified and scared of what had happened," Sophie said.

"Melita was too dangerous." Axelle examined her bloodred fingernails. "It wasn't safe to have her around. So the eleven remaining witches lay in wait for her. They were going to kill her."

I couldn't believe I was hearing this, that this was a real story, real history. And I couldn't believe the terrible conclusions my mind was leading me to. I glanced at Clio, who seemed as spellbound as I was.

"But it didn't work," Daedalus put in. "Melita was too strong even for the eleven together. She escaped and disappeared. No one ever saw her again."

"Before she left, she went back to the Source and the great cypress tree, where she'd performed the rite." Ouida took a deep breath, looking at her hands, folded in her lap. "She destroyed the tree, and the Source disappeared."

"Fast-forward fifteen years," said Manon. "By then it was obvious that the rite had had unexpected, lingering effects. None of the eleven was ever ill. Their magick was strong and clear and very, very powerful."

"Cerise's daughter, born that night, grew normally," Ouida said. "Oddly enough, she had the exact same birthmark that Cerise had had—a bright fleur-de-lis on her cheekbone. Somehow the magick that night had entered her as well, and her powers were unnaturally strong. Her name was Helène. In time she married and became with child. She died in childbirth, as her mother had. Her daughter Félice was marked with the fleur-de-lis."

My own birthmark felt like it was burning against my skin.

"Félice grew to adulthood, married, and died in childbirth," Daedalus said flatly. "It was like Cerise's line was cursed because Cerise had died the night of the ritual."

"And it continued that way," Ouida said. "Cerise's line never died out completely. Each successive generation produced one child. Your mother, Clémence, was the twelfth generation of Cerise's line. You, my dears, are the thirteenth. In your line, the power is very strong. You two have the potential to be extremely powerful witches."

"Especially if we put our powers together," said Clio coolly.

Ouida frowned. "Well, I don't know about that. I guess, in theory. I haven't really heard of other identical twins being able to do that. Have you?" she asked Daedalus.

I worked hard to keep the shock off my face and to not look at Clio.

Daedalus looked thoughtful. "I can recall only two other sets of identical twins among our *famille*," he said. "In the first pair, a twin died in childhood, before his rite of ascension. I don't remember anything remarkable about the other set."

"You must remember," Jules pointed out, "that only the eleven that took part in Melita's dark rite became, well, super-powerful. The rest of the community practiced *Bonne Magie* and were strong witches, but not supernaturally so. And of the eleven, you two are the first and only set of twins in any line."

I tried to look calm and interested. This was completely the opposite of what Petra had told us. They were lying. They wanted us to feel safe as twins. They

245

didn't realize that we'd already figured out someone was trying to harm us.

"What happened to the other eleven lines?" I asked.

"That brings us to the next important part of our story," said Daedalus. He stood before the fireplace, hands clasped behind his back. "You see—and this is the remarkable part—in addition to having incredibly strong magickal powers after that rite, in addition to never becoming ill and having injuries heal quickly, there was another unmistakable legacy granted to those who had drunk from the Source that night."

"They never . . . aged." Richard's voice was characteristically bitter.

My hands started to tremble, and I clasped them together tightly. *No, no, oh no . . .*

"What do you mean?" Clio asked tightly.

Richard looked at her. "They never aged. Have you not figured this out yet, Clio? As smart as you are?" he asked mockingly.

Ouida smiled sadly. "A woman named Claire is the village outcast. Marcel is the innocent young man."

I felt cold through and through, and the knuckles on my fingers were white. "Petra . . . she isn't really our grandmother, is she?" I asked.

Ouida shook her head. "No, not your grandmother. She's your ancestor, though. You see, Petra was Melita and Cerise's mother. That night she saw one daughter die and her other revealed as a power-mad monster. She's been helping the descendents of Cerise's line ever since. Though Clio was the first child she actually raised herself."

I looked over at Luc. "Don't tell me," I said, sounding as cool and smooth as a stone. "You're the heartless rake."

He made a gesture with his hand and looked away, looking tired and almost ill. Which I guessed was impossible—the ill part.

"Let me get this straight," said Clio. "You are the original eleven. You're saying you are *immortal.*"

Eight heads nodded with various levels of enthusiasm.

"I mean, so far, at least," Richard said.

How could this possibly be true?

"Okay, fine," said Clio briskly. "You guys are immortal, my grandmother isn't my grandmother, I understand why my mom died. But why did you want to find me and Thais? Get us together?"

"Because you would complete the Treize," said Daedalus. "As we said earlier."

"And that's important why?" Clio asked, her eyebrows raised.

"So we can re-create the rite, of course," said Jules. "Then you can be immortal too."

Uh . . . okay. I found my voice. "Why do you care if we're immortal?"

"He would get something out of it," Luc said, his voice as dry as bone. "Everyone would. Doing the rite would conjure up a huge amount of power—power that could be twisted and shaped to do anything anyone wanted it to. For example, we seem to be incapable of having children. We could change that. Or we could increase even the power we already have. If we reopen the Source, we can save people we . . . love. Save their lives."

Jules and Sophie shifted uneasily in their seats. Daedalus seemed coldly angry, a muscle in his jaw twitching as he watched Luc. Luc looked directly at me, and I found myself unable to tear my gaze away. "And some of us," he went on quietly, "are tired of immortality. And we would like to die."

Epilogue

The airplane intercom crackled. "Ladies and gentlemen, we're experiencing a bit of turbulence. At this time, please put your tray and seat in their upright and locked positions. Please make sure your seat belt is securely fastened. The captain has put on the 'remain seated' light, so do not move about the cabin until the light is turned off. Thank you."

Petra turned off her small overhead light and sat with her hands in her lap. Flashes of lightning illuminated the dark night outside, and horizontal lashes of rain streaked across her window. The plane suddenly dropped several feet, and a woman gave a short cry of alarm. A baby started crying.

It began to feel like a roller-coaster ride, with sudden, jarring jumps and drops and general shuddering in between. Across the aisle, a woman started praying out loud.

Petra closed her eyes, cleared her mind of everything, and began to murmur a general calming spell under her breath. Into the airplane cabin she sent soothing tendrils of calm and serenity, easing fears, cooling raw nerves, blunting the sharp edges of fear and panic.

She didn't bother with a protection spell for the plane. She knew it would be all right.

Ten minutes later, the atmosphere inside the cabin had achieved a lulling sense of divine reassurance. The man next to Petra gave her a small smile when another bolt of lightning cracked outside.

"Nature's fireworks," he said.

"Yes," Petra agreed. In fact, Petra was deeply afraid. Not for herself—that was pointless. Nor for the plane and its occupants, whom she knew to be safe. No, Petra was afraid of what might be happening below, 1500 miles away, back in New Orleans. Despite leaving Ouida in charge, Petra felt her base of power in danger of eroding.

The sooner she got back to New Orleans, the better. She had almost finished her mission: Thais would come to live with her, and Petra could keep an eye on both twins. Then she would try to formulate more of a plan, quickly. One that would take the twins away, keep them out of the Treize's long reach. Right now, only one thing stood between the twins and certain danger, possibly even death. That one thing was Petra.

She hoped she was up for the task.